"*Little One* is a charmingly quiet tale of the supernatural in which the human heart prevails over darkness, human beings matter when other things cannot, and we truly care about the protagonist. Huguenin is a writer to watch."

— Bruce McAllister, author of *Dream Baby* and *The Village Sang to the Sea*

"Throw a broken woman into a haunted house full of secrets and you'll have Timothy G. Huguenin's *Little One*. This dark little tale has sorrow, romance, and much more."

— Mercedes M. Yardley, Bram Stoker Award-winning author of *Nameless*

"*Little One* is an absolutely wonderful book, totally captivating and gripping. One of the very best ghost stories I've ever read. Very highly recommended!"

— John R. Little, Bram Stoker Award-winning author of *Miranda*, *The Memory Tree*, and *Soul Mates*

"Once everything is revealed at the end of a pulse-pounding downhill run, you will be blown away... It will chill your bones and warm your heart!"

— *The Horror Review*

"*Little One* is a frostbitten chiller that takes the traditional haunted house tale into fresh and intriguing territory. Bundle up and dig in!"

— Mark Carver, author of *Nikolai the Penitent* and *Beast*

Little One

Timothy G. Huguenin

Cover design and key illustration by Ben Baldwin
Copyediting by David Gatewood
Formatting by Polgarus Studio

In fond memory of Miles Dean
Rest in peace
Montani Semper Liberi

I would have been a beautiful woman by now. But when a body turns to dust before its time—when the mold is broken early—the spirit, like a casting, takes the mold's last form. Though my awareness has grown—in ways it would not have, had it still been bound by mortal flesh—I retain the likeness by which I was last known: a girl of six years.

Yes, though few who have seen me would know it, I have grown. I have learned.

My soul has not passed over because I have not yet let it. I have learned to become patient. Patience is a virtue, and I know I will taste the reward of its fulfillment. I am patiently awaiting my passing over, but I must have one thing before I am swept away by Elijah's fiery chariots.

I must have vengeance.

I feel that the time for vengeance is soon—though time is different for me now, as I am a soul unclothed, and not bound by time in the way that I once was.

The house I roam can feel vengeance's nearness, too. These dark rooms grow colder—colder even than winter's breath that frosts the windows.

I walk to one of these and look out at the white hills. I love these hills, especially in winter.

The wind outside moans through the trees, telling me that

my time is coming. It warns me to be careful, that vengeance is cold, too, and empty. But how can anyone trust the wind? Nobody knows where it comes from, or where it goes.

Vengeance will *be mine.*

Chapter One

Kelsea Stone looked out the window of the airliner and saw nothing but a floor of dark clouds below the stars. She sighed. She had been hoping for some city lights below, any spread of urban luminescence reminding her that her world would be waiting for her until she returned.

No such comfort. She was going where there were more trees than traffic. She had left LA, land of eternal light, and the light had turned its back on her.

She leaned back in her chair and shut her eyes. Surely there would be lights in Charleston. There was an airport, after all. But Charleston was not her final destination. The lawyer, James, had said it would be a three- to four-hour drive from West Virginia's state capital to Davis.

"We're out in the middle of nowhere," he had said over the phone. He had a slight accent, but not nearly as thick as Kelsea had expected. This man was educated, after all. She supposed even hick towns needed lawyers.

"It's a beautiful little mountain town. Highest town in West Virginia, you know. Very peaceful. You'll love it here."

"Should I bring a toothbrush, or would that be out of place?" she had joked.

James didn't laugh. "It's a different way of life out here, for sure. But you'll find that we're not all as backward as most folks assume. This is your home, too, you know."

Home? Maybe it was where she had been born, but it wasn't *home*. Home was bustle and rush hour. Home was street tacos and pitifully annoying mimes. Freaks and homeless and artists and teachers and bankers, Hispanics and Asians and Arabs and blacks and whites. Home was the city, where she could assimilate into the kaleidoscope of people and lights and sounds, become one with the multitude. Anonymity was her home.

"I'll meet you at the airport and drive you the rest of the way. Oh, and pack a hat and coat. Some boots, if you got 'em. I know it's seventy degrees there in LA, but it's still winter out here."

Even now, searching for memories of her past—something she rarely dared to do—she remembered none of her short life in West Virginia. Those first six years held nothing but blackness, like the clouds outside her window. Even the years after that, bouncing around foster homes, were hazy; she barely even thought of those days anymore. As soon as she was old enough, she had moved out west, running as far from her murky past as she could. She was thirty-one now, and she thought she had put it all behind her.

Now she was going back.

She closed her eyes and saw the city lights. The drone of the jet engine lulled her to sleep.

~

James was waiting for her with a sign that read "Kelsea S." and a smile as white as the paperboard in his hands. Kelsea was struck by how attractive he was. A dusting of black stubble softened a prominent jawline. His broad shoulders filled out a thick green wool coat over red-and-black checkered flannel. His indigo jeans weren't overly tight, but stretched just enough in all the right places.

Looks more like a lumberjack than a lawyer, Kelsea thought.

"Kelsea Stone?"

"That's me. And, um, James, right?"

"Yup. James Pendleton." He stuck out a hand, and she shook it. His grip was firm and cool. She was embarrassed to find herself caught in his soft blue eyes for a few seconds longer than was polite. She looked away and blushed.

"Wow, you really look…" He stopped midsentence and looked down at her bag. "I see your luggage came through all right. You ready? I'm parked outside."

She followed him out of the tiny airport. He led her to a black pickup—a Ford F-250. She laughed.

"What?"

"Nothing. It's just, I was expecting something a little more… I don't know. Lawyery."

"Hey, these are my fancy wheels," James said, smiling as he got in. "You should see my *fun* truck."

Kelsea put her luggage in the back of the cab and hoisted herself up into the passenger seat.

"So, I guess you don't remember me, do you?" James said as he drove.

Kelsea fidgeted in her seat. "Sorry, no. I really don't remember any of it, really. Not even, uh, *them*."

"You know, your mom and dad weren't perfect. But they were good people, all in all. Good to me, leastways. But I guess I understand how you feel."

Kelsea didn't say anything. How could he truly understand? She wasn't even sure *she* understood how she felt—or if she felt anything at all. How should you feel about a man and a woman whose faces you don't even know, who didn't keep you around? She had never learned why they had put her up for adoption, why she had never really felt a part of any family for any part of her life.

"Oh, hey," James said. "Out your window."

She looked. A yellow dome was lit up in the night, a beacon burning bright against the black sky.

"Beautiful, huh? The entire dome is plated with real gold. Normally when I travel, I fly out of Pittsburgh, or sometimes DC. But I told you to meet me here because I wanted you to see this."

"It's really something."

She watched the lights of Charleston shrink in the mirror as they fled the city.

~

Within a couple of hours, the road had whittled itself down from wide interstate to a narrow, winding two-lane where the snow-dusted trees crowded in. The moon was hidden by the clouds, so even when there were breaks in the trees, it was hard to see the landscape past the boundary of the truck's headlights.

We're on the back end of Nowhere, Kelsea thought.

Though there were patches of snow and ice on the road, James didn't seem to be worried. He drove with speed and confidence around the curves, even when the guardrail was perilously close. Kelsea began to feel queasy.

"I'm not feeling too good."

James looked over at her, surprised. "Sorry. Don't worry, I'll stop for gas soon. You can get some fresh air. You gonna be okay for a few minutes?"

Kelsea nodded. She wondered where there might be a gas station in this wilderness.

The trees thinned out, and almost out of nowhere they came to an Exxon surrounded by a sparse smattering of buildings. A used car lot with a handful of snow-covered junkers was across the road from a billboard warning against transporting bug-infested firewood.

This seemed to be the main street of the town, if you could call it that. Kelsea looked around for other signs of life, but there wasn't much going on.

"Is this it?" she asked James.

"No, this here's Harman. We're close. We'll be at your folks' old place in no time."

James had been running the heater the whole time, and although she had seen the snow out her window, Kelsea was unprepared for the cold that hit her when she got out of the truck to stretch her legs. She wrapped her hands around her shoulders and shivered. Her breath made thick blue clouds in front of her face. She smelled smoke from the fireplaces of the few houses nearby.

"Jesus, it's *freezing*."

James looked over from the pump. "I told you, it's not Los Angeles weather. You did bring a coat, right?"

Kelsea nodded. "It's in my suitcase."

James just chuckled as he topped off the tank. She suddenly realized she was staring at him and that her eyes had settled on the upper backside of his jeans. She turned away and hoped he hadn't noticed. The machine spit out a receipt, and they got back in.

"Your stomach feeling any better?" James asked.

"Yeah. It's hard to be nauseous when your body is a block of ice."

He laughed as he started the truck and continued down the slippery road.

Unbelievably, the road became even narrower and more winding for a while before they broke free of the trees and the road straightened out. The clouds had parted, and the moon revealed a quiet, snow-covered landscape surrounded by rounded mountains, everything soft and lumpy and white. It was like they were driving across the top of a foamy cappuccino. Kelsea gasped.

"Canaan Valley, West Virginia," James said. He pronounced *Canaan* with the accent on the second syllable, a long *a* sound. "Most beautiful place you'll ever lay eyes on. You oughta see it in the fall. Leaves so bright, you wouldn't believe it. Like the mountains are bleeding and on fire at the same time."

They turned onto an unmarked road covered in a thick layer of packed snow. James shifted into four-wheel drive and followed the road into a thick section of woods. He turned down a driveway. A wooden sign fixed to a post next to the mailbox read:

Hendricks's Place

Above the name, somebody had scratched the word *CRAZY* in rough, zigzagging capital letters.

Great, Kelsea thought. *So my parents were insane.*

Past the sign, surrounded by trees and topped with snow, was a large, two-story house with an A-frame front.

"Here we are," James said.

James set the brake, and they hopped out of the truck. Kelsea's tennis shoes crunched in the snow.

She took a moment to take it in. A deck wrapped around the house. The building's wooden shiplap exterior was stained a dark walnut that looked black on the fringes of the headlights' illumination. A stone chimney rose from the middle of the roof where the A-frame joined the wider part of the house.

Though Kelsea thought it was a beautiful structure, even in the low light she could see signs of disrepair. Shingles were buckling and missing from the roof in a few areas. Cracks ran across many of the smaller windows. Some of the deck's railing supports leaned this way and that like crooked teeth. These things, combined with the night's darkness and the shadows cast by the truck's headlights, set Kelsea's nerves on edge. She felt a slight twist in her stomach.

"What do you think?" James said.

It's creepy, she thought. But she wasn't going to say that out loud. She struggled for an answer she could give him.

"It's, um… confusing."

"Confusing?"

"Yeah, well. It's like… I assumed that my parents, they must have had *some* reason to give me up. I guess I assumed since they lived in West Virginia… all you ever hear, you know…"

"You thought they were poor, right?"

"Well, yeah. I mean, it obviously needs some work, but this is a nice house. Way more than a few steps up from a singlewide. Had they always owned it?"

"They moved in about a year before you were born."

A surge of anger heated Kelsea's face. If her parents hadn't given her up for adoption because of financial difficulties, then *why*? She glared at the house, and she felt it scowl back at her.

"Well, it's cold out here," James said, "and I'm tired of standing. I have the key, if you want to stay in it tonight."

"I booked a room for tonight. Wasn't sure what to expect. Do you know where, uh, the Black Bear is?"

"Sure thing. It's about ten minutes from here. You can get a good rest and I'll drive you back here in the morning. Probably good thinking; I've got the heat turned way down in there, and it'd take a while to warm it up. Probably would be a chilly night for you, at least for a bit."

They got back in the truck. Neither of them spoke until they got to Kelsea's suite.

James carried Kelsea's luggage to her room. "I have some paperwork I need to take care of in the morning," he said, "but I can be here around ten, if that works for you."

"Sure. I'll see you then."

I see them out the window; the light from their vehicle shines through me. I don't think they notice my presence, but I slip to the edge of the cracked and frosted glass, just to be sure. I don't wish to be seen yet. It's not quite time.

They return to their truck and back down the driveway. They turn around outside the gate. The tires spin a bit in the snow and then catch, and they leave for the highway.

The physical sensations that come with emotions when you are still encased in flesh don't just fly away when your body fails. They do change, but they don't grow fainter. They're different. Elevated. They are pure, I think.

I feel pure rage boiling in me where my belly used to be.

I release my anger on a shelf of books, pulling it down and ripping the books and tearing the pages and breaking the spines. It hurts to let loose this anger, but it also feels good.

Once, not long before my physical life was cut short, a doctor had to lance a throbbing, swollen wound I had on my little finger. I cried when the doctor cut me, but when the pus ran out, I felt relief.

This feels like that.

I can only imagine how great the relief will be when I finally unleash this wrath on the one to whom it's due. I remember that I need to save some of my fury for then, and I stop with the books.

It's funny, the habits you keep after you die. Even though I have no lungs, I am panting now as pages from The Count of Monte Cristo *float down, around and through my spirit.*

Edmond Dantes is a hero of mine. I've read his story at least ten thousand times since my death.

(Reading came easy for me after I was separated from my frail child's brain. As I've said before, losing your shell allows your awareness to expand in ways you'll never know—until it happens to you.)

I may not have the wealth that Dantes had at his disposal when he fulfilled his mission of vengeance upon his enemies, but I do have the patience and the sense of purpose.

It does not bother me that I have destroyed this book, or any of the others. Books are physical things, fleshly things, like my old body that lies decayed in a box. The stories those books contained—they are in my soul, and they can't be destroyed.

Can a soul be destroyed? I wonder.

Leave me now. Sometimes it tires me to go on like this to you.

Chapter Two

Kelsea woke up in her clothes from the night before. She looked at her phone for the time. She hadn't had cell service since sometime before getting here, but her battery hadn't died.

It was almost nine thirty. James had said he would get there at ten. She showered quickly, toweled off, threw on some clothes, and applied some mascara and other basics. She wasn't the type of girl that needed a lot of makeup, but she liked to be safe about these things, especially with that lumbersexual lawyer coming to pick her up at any minute.

What's gotten into you? she scolded herself. *The last thing you need right now is a relationship, especially a long-distance thing with some hick from the sticks, lawyer or no.*

Still, he *was* kind of a hunk. And she supposed it wouldn't hurt to make herself presentable, even desirable, if she could. Show him what a sophisticated, southern California woman looked like. Maybe he would move to LA, start a practice out west, maybe they could spend some time together—nothing serious, of course, nothing that would get in the way of her career...

She shook her head. *This is ridiculous.*

There was a knock at the door.

"Ms. Stone?" James's voice came from outside the suite.

"Just a sec."

She applied some finishing touches, hurriedly crammed everything back into her bag, and opened the door. James was standing there in a new shade of plaid under the green coat he had been wearing last night. He had shaved, showing off a cleft in his chin and dimples in his smile.

Yeah, maybe it doesn't hurt a girl to dream a bit.

"Have you eaten breakfast yet?" he said. "I thought we might take a ride into town for something. It's the opposite way, but I'm starving, and the cereal at my house just wasn't going to cut it."

"Sounds fine. I could use some good coffee, if this town of yours has anything decent."

"I think I know a place."

~

Kelsea watched in vain for signs of a city as James drove them out of Canaan. "So where is this place?" she asked.

"There are two main towns up here on the mountain," James said. "Davis and Thomas. Actually, in Canaan you still have a Davis zip code, even though we're a ways out. The coffee shop is in Thomas. TipTop. I think you'll like it."

Kelsea saw a few restaurants and shops as James drove through Davis—definitely more going on here than in Harman—but before she knew it the whole town was in their rearview mirror. It was not even a speck compared to LA.

A few minutes later they entered Thomas, which was about the same size. James parked on the main street, where a frozen river ran along one side of the road, and a line of old brick storefronts faced them on the other. A sign above one door showed a cartoon hot air balloon floating between the words *Tip* and *Top*.

James led her inside. They ordered, then sat down at a table alongside the wall. Kelsea sipped her latte as she took the place in. It had a trendy, bohemian feel that surprised her. A large, metal, mixed media artwork sunburst hung from the wall above a shelf packed with bags of fair trade coffees, herbal teas, bottles of wine, and local handmade pottery. Paintings and photographs on canvas populated a wall adjacent to the small wooden table where she and James sat.

A woman about Kelsea's age with blond dreadlocks sat at another table talking to a full-bearded twenty-something guy. A few friends dressed in ski apparel laughed over americanos across the room. A teen wearing a Baja hoodie striped in Rasta colors walked into the store and began chatting with the barista.

If Kelsea didn't know better, this could be just another hipster coffee joint in LA, with the exception that everyone in here was Caucasian.

"So, what do you think?" James said. He ate his breakfast sandwich in big bites, but he was careful to swallow before he talked.

"It's not what I expected, honestly," she said. "I don't know, I guess I was thinking there would be, you know…" She trailed off, not sure if what she had almost said would offend him.

"More rednecks, right?" He smiled. "Sure, we have plenty of those. You'll see some in here from time to time, too. Still, there are a lot of old folks that are angry about all the so-called 'hippies' that have been moving here. But hey, we need as much business as we can get to survive, whoever's money it is. Most of the economy is tourism these days. People are coming around to the changes, mostly."

"So, which camp are you?" She took a bite of her cinnamon bun. It melted in her mouth. "Redneck, or hippie, or what?"

James laughed. "I grew up in Canaan. Parents were pretty well-off. So I guess, neither. But I do remember both Davis and Thomas before they started getting so, uh, I don't know. *Artsy*. I never really took sides, though. I reckon you might consider me sort of a rich hillbilly. We hillbillies are a more complicated bunch than you think."

Kelsea nodded and made some more progress on her cinnamon bun. "So, like, do I need to sign any papers or anything?" she said. "Is the house mine, or do I, I don't know… Do I need to do something to claim it?"

"Your folks hired me to be executor, so I've handled most of the boring stuff. House is yours. I'll give you the deed when we get to my house."

"Cool."

"So what's your plan? If you don't mind me asking."

Kelsea sipped on her latte. "I don't know yet. I suppose I'll sell the place. I haven't decided if I wanted to go through the house myself or have someone else clean it for me. My flight for LA is in a week. I figure that'll give me enough time to look through most of the stuff if I want to, and find a good real estate agent."

"All right, fair enough. I know it's none of my business, but a lot of people find this place a great vacation area. I'm sure you'll have no problem selling it for that reason, but at the same time, it might be something you want to hold on to for a while. You never know. You may want to come back here sometime. But hey." James put his hands up. "That's just me. I've lived here almost my whole life. I love it. Maybe it's not for you. Still, something to consider."

"Sure, I'll think about it."

There was a silence. She looked down and stared at her drink. She felt awkward in the lull, but James seemed to take comfort in it.

He finally broke it. "I was thinking you probably don't want me to chauffeur you around the whole time. Your parents had a vehicle, but it's pretty old. I have it in the shop right now. There's a car rental place about a half hour away, but I was thinking I could save you some money and loan you one of my trucks."

"That really would be great, thanks."

"Don't mention it. My place isn't far from the house. I'll take you there and get you all set up."

They finished their food and stood from the table. James threw a few bills down next to his empty mug.

"James?"

"Yeah?"

"You knew my parents, right?"

"Sure. They were good to me. In a way, I think of them a bit like family, you know."

"I just…" Kelsea couldn't finish, surprised that it was so hard to talk about them. She had never thought that much about her parents before, didn't think it should be such a big deal to ask him about them now that she was inheriting their house. But for whatever reason, at that moment she lost her nerve. "Never mind."

~

James drove them to his house, which was a few miles off of the main road through Canaan. It was a gorgeous, well-kept log house with big windows, similar in design to Kelsea's parents' house, but not so big as to seem too pretentious for a bachelor. He put the truck in park next to a larger one in his snowy gravel driveway.

"Okay," he said, leaving the engine running. "I have some things to do. You'll be okay by yourself?"

"Sure, thanks." Kelsea tried to smile politely, though the question annoyed her. Of course she would be okay. She was a grown woman.

"Great. You saw the way we came, right? Follow back until you get to 32, then turn right, like you're going back toward town. Stay on that for about four miles. You remember where we turned last night? Coming from this way, it'll be on the right, just before the park entrance. There's no sign, but if you look close you should see the turn. If you're on the right road, you'll see the sign for your driveway about a half mile in. Any problems, just backtrack and I'll be here working."

"I think I got it. Thanks a lot, James."

"No problem. Oh, by the way, you should know there's a lot of firewood out behind the house, but it also has gas-powered central heating. I went through and made sure the gas and other utilities were on and working last week so it would be ready for you, but I left the thermostat turned way down so you wouldn't be surprised with too much extra on your bills. I would turn that up as soon as I got in, if I were you. The fireplace is nice to look at, but the house is too big for it to heat all the outer rooms."

Kelsea nodded. They both stepped out of the truck, and Kelsea walked around to the driver's side. Out of the corner of her eye she noticed him checking her out. She felt her face turn pink and tried to hold back a smile. Normally this kind of thing irritated her, but now for some reason she found herself liking the attention.

"Oh, hold on a second." James ran inside, then came back out after a minute with a large orange envelope in his hand. "Here's the deed to the house." He handed it to her. "Good luck. Watch out for deer; they're everywhere here. Like I said, just come back this way if you need anything. If you want, we could go to town and get dinner this evening. My treat, of course."

"Sure, thanks. That would be great."

James's blue eyes lit up. "Awesome. I'll come by around five and pick you up. Oh, almost forgot!" James fumbled through his jacket pockets until he pulled out a key. He handed it to her. "Here you go! The key to your new house."

"Thanks." She put the key in her purse.

Kelsea got into the truck, and James headed toward his front door. He turned around halfway and waved at her. Kelsea waved back as she pulled out.

Did I just agree to a date? she thought as she left.

~

Kelsea parked in front of the A-frame and stepped out of the truck into the cold, gray day. Two deer on the edge of the woods turned their snow-white tails up at her and bounded away.

In the cloudy morning light, the house didn't have quite the unnerving effect she had felt the night before. It was a nice place, really. Sure, it needed some work—even as she thought it, she noticed some places where the siding needed repairs—but it was a beautiful building. This could definitely make a good home for somebody. Not for her, of course. One week in this dark, cell service-less neck of the woods would be all the West Virginia Kelsea would ever need. But with the right kind of work and a good real estate agent, she could see this place bringing in a nice bit of extra cash.

As she walked toward the deck's front steps, she thought she saw movement in one of the house's windows. She stopped and peered, but the inside of the house was dark, and there was frost obscuring any good view through the window.

There better not be raccoons or something living in there, Kelsea thought.

She walked up the steps to the front door. Mounted in its center was a dark metal door knocker shaped like a bear. She traced its texture with her fingers. It was cold and stung her skin. She swung the knocker, and it made a loud clacking noise against itself.

A gust of wind whistled through the trees and made her tense up. She pulled the key from her purse and unlocked the deadbolt. The knob turned stiffly, and the door seemed stuck in its frame when she pushed it. She gave it some shoulder, and it opened.

Kelsea returned the key to her purse and stepped inside. Gray light came in through the tall windows, but the air was cold, and her breath formed thick smoke-like clouds. She shut the door behind her and set the deed and her purse on a small table next to the door. She pulled her phone from her purse and checked it, just in case. Still no service. She sighed and put it in her back pocket.

The thermostat and light switch were both on the wall across from the door. She walked over and flipped both on. She heard the heat kick in as she pushed the slider on the thermostat up to seventy degrees.

"That should do it," she said.

She looked around. She was in a high-ceilinged living room with a chandelier made from deer antlers. The floors were hardwood, with a large oval rug in the center. The walls were also wood, except where the stone fireplace and chimney ascended. A leather sofa sat near the fireplace, and

21

on the other side, the living room became an open kitchen. Above the kitchen was a balcony—some kind of loft.

Kelsea stepped over to the fireplace. A buck's head with a ten-point spread protruded from the stonework above. Its brown glass eyes stared down at her.

"Well, you're kind of freaky," she said to it.

Picture frames were lined up on the mantel, and she took one down. It showed a couple—Kelsea's birth parents, she presumed—probably in their fifties, posing together on the deck in front of the house. The man's hair and beard was gray, with some streaks of black trying to hang on for another year or so. The woman was a little taller than the man, with white hair and eyes green like a tropical reef. Both were incredibly thin, almost to the point of gauntness. Neither of them was smiling; their faces possessed a sadness that somehow both robbed from and added to their beauty at the same time.

Kelsea saw herself in both of them, but most of her looks had apparently come from the woman.

She set the picture back on the mantel and pulled down another. It showed the same couple, but decades younger, full-bodied and healthy. They leaned against the deck's side railing with the woods in the background. The sun was shining, and the trees behind them were full-leafed and verdant.

The resemblance between Kelsea and the woman in this photo was striking. Her hair was the color of bright honey, straight and soft. Long, tanned legs stretched from denim shorts. Her face was turned with a loving look toward her husband, whose smile was white, wide, and infectious. His wavy jet black hair was slightly ruffled, blowing in a breeze.

One side of the photograph, beside the woman, looked ragged, as if part of the photo had been torn off. Kelsea looked closer. The woman's arm stretched down, and in her hand, just before the tear was the tiny hand of someone else.

That's my *hand!*

Despite the cold of the room, Kelsea felt her face heat up. They had ripped her out of the photograph? But *why*?

She screamed and threw the picture to the floor. The wooden frame cracked open, and the glass shattered.

"Why? Why did you send me away?" she yelled at the ceiling. She began to cry. "What did I ever do to you? Was I so much of a burden?"

She fell to her knees and wept with her face in her hands.

~

Kelsea hadn't expected this place to carry so much emotional weight. She was exhausted from crying, and on top of that, the house was starting to get warm, making her desperate for a nap. She left the living room and walked halfway down a hallway to a staircase. She ascended and headed down another hallway, finding a broom closet first, then a bathroom.

Finally she found a bedroom. The bedding smelled weird and was coated in a thin layer of dust, but she didn't care. She could barely keep her eyes open. She lay down on the soft mattress and fell asleep.

She's here now. She can't see or hear you. But she can *discover me, if I'm not careful. I may be a spirit, an outcast between realms, but I'm still somehow tethered to this house and visible to these people until my time to move on. You, however, well… What are you, this consciousness unbound, floating freely and undetected across minds and places and times? How do you remain unseen by the living, still reserving your ability to observe all these things?*

I'm not yet ready to make myself known. There is still some waiting to do. Still some time before even she *will be ready.*

When she arrived, just a couple hours ago, I wasn't sure what to think. I got my first good look at her when she stepped out of the truck. Her hair, so long and golden, and her eyes, sparkling emeralds. She is beautiful.

Such beauty—beauty that was stolen from me too early—makes me angry again. I want to tear down more books, but she would hear.

Though I was scared, I kept trying to catch glances of her after she came inside. When she was crying, I stole a view of her reflection in the living room window.

Even when she cries, she is beautiful.

When she walked down the hall, I peeked around the corner after she passed.

Now she is sleeping, and I stand here by her bedside and watch her.

Her beauty awakens more anger and jealousy in me, but at the same time, I can't look away. She is captivating. I am certain that you would feel the same, if you were in my place. Look at her yourself and see. You understand, don't you?

But be quiet. I don't want her to awake now and see me. If I reveal myself too soon, she won't be ready for what I've done. Reconciliation will come, at the end, if she wants it. I know that they *want it, but they won't get it until I release them—and I won't let that happen until I first get my vengeance.*

Chapter Three

Kelsea woke to a rumbling stomach. She pulled her phone from her pocket to check the time. All she saw was a blank screen. The battery had run out.

She groaned. Her charging cord was in her luggage, in the truck. She didn't want to go out into the cold again.

She sat up and yawned. The sky outside the cracked window was still covered in a gray blanket, so she couldn't make a guess on the hour based on how high the sun was.

It's past lunch o'clock, whatever it is.

She left the bedroom and walked back down the hallway. She stopped in the bathroom and smoothed back hair that had been mussed from the pillow.

While she was looking in the mirror, she thought she saw the door close slightly behind her. She turned around.

"Hello?" She stuck her head out into the hall. Nobody was there. "James? Are you in here?"

No answer.

Weird. Maybe a draft coming through. Or—

She remembered the movement she had seen in the

window when she was outside.

Not an animal. Oh, please, not an animal.

She looked up and down the hall for signs of life other than her own—rat poop, animal scratches, something.

Animals leave scratches, right? Like rubbings? And claw marks? Yeah, I think probably they would.

If there was something living in the house, she didn't see a trace of it. She sighed and walked down to the living room.

"You can't hide forever," she said. "Mr. Deer and I are keeping an eye out. We'll find you."

She winked at Mr. Deer, then went out to the truck.

The day hadn't gotten much warmer, and the sudden contrast between the now well-heated house interior and the winter weather outside shocked her. She ran to the truck and pulled her suitcase out as fast as she could. She extended the top handle and tried rolling it behind her, but it stuck in the snow.

"Come on!"

She pushed the handle down, picked up the bag by its side handle, and ran to the front door.

The door didn't open.

"That's right, you're a stubborn one," she said. She set the suitcase down and gathered herself. She turned the handle again, and this time she put her weight into the door like she had earlier.

It didn't move.

She tried again, harder. Nothing. The door was locked.

"You've got to be *kidding* me!" She checked her pocket, but as she feared, the key wasn't there. She pressed her face up to one of the tall windows next to the door and saw her purse sitting right there on the table where she had left it.

How can the door be locked? she thought. *It's a bolt. It doesn't just lock automatically when you close it.*

She was really feeling the cold now, so she opened her suitcase, dug out her jacket, and pulled it on. It wasn't designed for extended winter use; while it took the edge off of the cold, when the wind blew, it still cut straight to her bone.

She walked around the wraparound deck looking for another way in. A pair of glass French doors led into the back of the house, but these, too, were locked.

"I don't have time for this bullshit," she said, teeth chattering.

She looked out at the back yard that was covered in thick snow. A mix of deciduous and evergreen trees demarcated the edge of the yard, thickening into a dark forest past the border. Just on this side of the trees was a ragged shed, with piles of firewood stacked outside of it. A scraggly apple tree sprawled out from the snow in the middle of the yard, its bare fingers scratching at the dull sky. An old rope and tire swing hung from one of its bony branches and swung in the wind.

A nostalgic and sorrowful pang surprised Kelsea upon seeing the swing, though no memory came to mind that could explain it.

She continued to circle the house, following the deck all the way around to the opposite front corner. One of the windows with the spider-web cracks looked like it was a tiny bit open. She jammed her fingers into the gap beneath it and pushed up. It wouldn't budge.

She remembered a toolbox in the bed of James's truck. She ran to the truck, hopped into the bed, and lifted the toolbox's heavy corrugated metal lid. Among the motley pile of tools inside it, she found a crowbar.

"Yes!" She held it up and thanked the redneck gods for this strange place called West Virginia, where even the lawyers drove pickup trucks full of tools.

She looked back at the house. She thought she saw another movement, this time behind the window that she was planning on opening. Suddenly she felt a little less victorious and much more hesitant to go back inside.

Maybe that's where the animals are hiding, she thought.

She pulled herself together. She would have to take on the rodents, or raccoons, or whatever was living in her new house, sooner or later. Might as well be now.

How bad could it be, anyway? It's not like a family of bears would take up residence in a dead couple's house. I mean, I don't think *bears would do that. Right?*

She gripped the crowbar tightly, thinking of it more as a weapon now than a tool, and trudged warily to the window. She rubbed some snow and frost off the glass and looked through with hands cupped around her face. With all the cracks running through the glass, it was hard to make much out, but she could see that there were papers all over the floor. If an animal really *was* living in the house, this looked to be the room where it had made its nest.

Kelsea gulped, then moved to put the crowbar into the gap between the window and the frame. Only, the gap was no longer there. The window was completely shut.

That's weird. I'm sure this was the one.

She checked the other windows near her, in case she had gotten mixed up, but none of them were open at all.

It must have slipped and closed itself when I was looking for the tool, Kelsea thought. But how could that have been, considering how stuck the window was when she had tried to open it before?

She forced the crowbar into the wood at the base of the window and heaved. It moved about half a centimeter, then stopped and refused to move any further. She peered through the glass—and saw where the lock was holding the window shut.

I know *this thing wasn't locked before,* she thought. *It was too far open for that.* But she had no other explanation.

The trees sang lowly as a sharp wind chilled her. She looked at the fissures in the glass. *Well, I'm going to have to replace most of these windows anyway*, she thought, and she broke the pane with the crowbar.

Little sharp triangles remained around the edges. Kelsea cleared these stragglers away with a few more knocks of the crowbar. Then she climbed inside, careful not to step on the remains of the broken window that was now on the floor.

She jumped when she saw a black bear standing in a corner of the room, raring up and baring its teeth.

It's stuffed, you idiot. She put a hand on her chest and laughed nervously.

The room was some kind of study. Bookshelves and hunting trophies covered the walls, though many of the books had been pulled down, and pages littered the floor, forming the possible animal nest. A writing desk was buried in papers and books off to one side, with a wall-mounted telephone above it. *Don't see those much anymore.*

The room smelled of old books and pipe tobacco. No animal odors of any kind—but she wasn't taking any chances. Kelsea stepped carefully around the pile of books and torn pages in the center of the floor. If something was nesting inside of that mess, she didn't want to step on it. She watched the pile for a full minute with the crowbar ready as cold air poured in from the broken window. Some of the pages rustled in the wind, but nothing moved underneath.

She was only partially satisfied that there was no animal in that mess—at least right *now*—but there was no point just standing here. Besides, she was freezing. She could only imagine what the missing window would do to her gas bill if she didn't cover it soon.

Exiting the room, she made her way back to the front door and pulled her suitcase inside out of the snow. She dug out her charger, hooked it up to her phone, and plugged it into the nearest outlet.

"Now, Mr. Deer," she said. "Where would you say I could find some cardboard or plastic or something for that window in the study?" She looked up at the mounted deer head, but he didn't answer. She laughed and shook her head. "Just one day in the boonies and I'm already talking to dead animals."

She ended up finding a folded, paint-stained, plastic drop cloth in the upstairs closet. She had seen a staple gun in

James's toolbox, so she went back out to the truck once more to replace her crowbar with the stapler. This time she took extra care to bring the house key along. She hooked it onto the truck's key ring so she would be sure not to lose track of it.

Tool in hand, she set to work sealing the window. The plastic was awkward to work with, especially since she didn't know where any scissors were. But she folded it a bunch of times and stapled it somewhat haphazardly to the inside of the window frame. The excess hung down in big flaps of painted plastic. The outside wind blew against the rigged plastic window and made a sound like a flag flapping. It still felt colder next to the window compared to the rest of the room, but it would be good enough until she got the glass replaced.

Kelsea tentatively poked through the mess of destroyed book remains on the floor. Nothing growled or scampered out from the pile. She poked a few more times, still not completely sure nothing was in there. She swept up the glass and dumped it into an empty wastebasket next to the writing desk.

She ran a finger across the desk's polished wooden surface, leaving a clean line in the settled dust. The desk chair's upholstery was faded and frayed. An image came to her of the man in the picture, her biological father, leaning back in the chair and smoking his pipe while he pondered life and writing. She wondered if this image came from a lost memory or just her imagination.

Her stomach growled. She wasn't going to get any less

hungry in here. She went to the kitchen.

The fridge was empty, of course. If any food had once been left in there, James would have thrown it all out a while ago. There wasn't much in the cupboards, either: some flour, a few boxes of expired cereal, and a small population of canned food. She didn't know what else she had expected, and she was actually relieved. She was starting to think she needed to warm up to this place in small doses, and catching lunch in town before getting some groceries to bring back here for the week was as good an excuse as any to get out.

As she took her phone from the charger, she looked up at Mr. Deer. "Maybe there will be cell service in town," she said. "A girl can dream, right?"

From the window, I watch her drive away. I'm unsure how to feel now. When she first stepped from the truck this morning, I hated her for her beauty. When she entered the house, I was fascinated. When she cried, I was angry with her for thinking that the history and dark memories of this house were only about her.

When she slept, I loved her.

Then she woke, and I was scared, and then I hated her and loved her and wondered about her all at once, and it confused me so that I was tired of looking at her.

So I locked her out.

I thought maybe she would drive away and leave me to brood in the solitude I hadn't known I loved so much until today. Or maybe she would stand there at the door, trying to get in, while the winter sucked at her soul until her body exhaled its spirit to join me in my roaming of this house. I wonder: what then would have happened to my plan for vengeance? What then would happen between her and them*? Would I still be able to hold them away until my vengeance was fulfilled?*

But it doesn't matter now. She still lives, and my plan will continue. And it seems that she needed to get away from here as much as I needed her to leave.

Good riddance! Her tallness, her womanliness, her pretty

long blond hair and green eyes and fancy leather purse and long eyelashes and full lips—she makes me sick; doesn't she make you sick? People like her, they always whine about life's unfairness. Look at them! Death—*that's what's unfair. Being stuck in this diminutive form, nothing but a wisp of breath shaped like a child, stretched thin by time and hate—that's the real injustice of this world. Waiting all this time—because it's up to me to make my own justice! They turned a blind eye to my cause, whatever higher powers may or may not exist beyond this gap I straddle between flesh and spirit.*

I hate her. I hate her I hate her!

Don't look at me like that! What do you know about me, or about justice, or about the dead? You can fly away from here if you wish and forget about my troubles as if they are nothing more than Dumas's fictional words, now spread all over the study floor. You know nothing of injustice until you know your own death at your friend's hand, and that former friend's prosperity after.

Go away from me now. I'm tired of company.

I said get out!

Chapter Four

It was taking Kelsea longer to get to Davis than she had expected. She could feel the truck wanting to fishtail around the curves, and the last thing she needed was to wreck James's vehicle, so she drove slowly. Another car caught up behind her and drove within a few feet of her tailgate.

"Come on, are you serious?" she said in the mirror. She honked her horn.

The driver behind her only honked back, longer and angrier. After a few minutes, he pulled out into the other lane and gunned it, tires spinning and car swerving slightly as he took the outside of a blind curve to get around her.

"Insane. Absolutely insane," Kelsea muttered. But she was glad that the driver had passed; now nobody was breathing down her neck. She hunkered down and stared at the white road, her hands making deep impressions on the steering wheel.

She finally took the last sharp bend, and the town of Davis appeared. She noticed the small grocery store on the right as she entered town. She would pick up some groceries after lunch.

Davis didn't have very many options in the way of lunch spots, it seemed. In fact, it didn't have much at all. Even though James had driven through the town with her once before, she was still surprised when the buildings disappeared not even a mile later. She considered driving the few more miles to Thomas, to that coffee place James had taken her in the morning, but she had seen a sign for burritos, and the less she drove in the snow, the better. She made a slow but nerve-wracking U-turn in the middle of the slippery road and drove back toward the restaurant.

Hellbender Burritos was small, but it wasn't very crowded, and the server quickly came and took her order. A few skiers trickled in while she waited for her burrito. Her phone started buzzing. She pulled it from her purse and watched the voicemails and texts pile up as the phone caught up with the few bars of cell service available in town.

She had a voicemail from Mark—Matthew? Mike?— some guy she had gone on a date with the week before, all sports and flash and no brains. She deleted it without listening. Most of her texts were from Marge, an editor at *Ensemble Weekly*, the entertainment magazine she wrote for. She had a few questions about how Kelsea's latest assignment was wrapping up. Kelsea had promised to finish it while she was here. She was just in the middle of texting her back when Marge called.

"Hey, Marge."

"Kelsea, God, I've been trying to get through to you for like two hours. I thought something had happened."

"Sorry. There's no service at the house. I just came into

town for lunch. It seems pretty spotty here, too."

"Well. I'm glad you're not dead. How's it going?"

"The house is kind of a mess. I really haven't gotten anything done with it yet." A waiter came with her burrito. Kelsea nodded her thanks.

"No, I mean with the story. You haven't responded to any of my emails."

"Oh, right. Sorry, I haven't had a chance. You know I got here late last night. I'll have to look at the emails tomorrow. There's wifi at the coffee shop, I think, but I forgot to bring my computer into town. I should be able to finish the piece tomorrow morning and email you the draft when I come into town again."

"Fab, Kels. Keep me posted."

"I'll do my best. But really, Marge, the cell service here is atrocious. Even right now your voice is pretty faint."

"Wow, and you're in the city and everything?"

"Well, I wouldn't call it a city. It's a really small town. Kind of quaint. Really quiet. Like, *really*. I'm in this burrito place for lunch, and there's like three other people in here, that's it. But you should see this burrito. It's massive. It could feed, like, a family of four."

"Right, well I'll let you get back to your lunch. Looking forward to that piece. *Ciao*."

"It'll be in your inbox soon. Later."

James's other pickup was parked outside when Kelsea returned to the house. She parked next to it, then quickly looked in the rearview mirror to check her hair before stepping out. She could hear the other truck's engine ticking as it cooled; James must have gotten here recently. She left her groceries in the back of the truck and walked inside.

"James?" she called. She shed her coat, tossed it on the couch, and shivered. The house was cold again; perhaps there was something wrong with the heater. *Good thing James is here. Maybe he can fix it or something.* "James? Where are you?"

She heard a crash of breaking glass and some sort of clanging sound down the hall, followed by a stream of curses.

"James, are you okay?"

Kelsea set her purse down and hurried toward the noise. She found James at the back of the house, in the room with the glass French doors. This room was even bigger than the living room, with space for a pool table, two couches, a TV, and several more bookshelves. Once again, many of the books were scattered on the floor.

James was hunched over in one corner, next to a grandfather clock. The glass panes protecting the clock's face and pendulum were broken. James was holding his forearm. It was bloodied, and his face was pale.

"James! What happened? I'll call an ambulance!" She turned to run for her phone.

"No, don't worry about it," James said. "It's a scratch. I just need something to stop the bleeding. Besides, I doubt your call would go through."

"Are you sure?"

"Yeah, just check the bathroom for a towel or something."

Kelsea ran to the bathroom and found some white hand towels stacked in a cabinet under the sink. She pulled the top one out and looked at it. It was covered in dust and some old rust stains from being up against the pipes. She dropped it and took the next towel, which was as clean as she could hope for, and ran back to James.

"Here," she said.

James pressed the towel against his bleeding arm. He leaned his back against the wall, closed his eyes, and breathed deeply.

"You sure you're okay?" Kelsea said.

"Yeah, I'll be fine." His eyes were still closed. "Just feeling a bit dizzy. Wow, I guess I lost a bit of blood on that clock."

Kelsea looked at the broken pieces of glass still attached to the front of the clock. Bright red blood dripped down the corners of the jagged shards like the clock itself was bleeding. Kelsea became lightheaded and nauseous at the sight of it. She sat down next to James.

He looked at her and smiled sheepishly. "Guess I should tell you. I may try to look all macho, but I'm kind of a klutz."

"What happened?"

"I came over to see if you were doing okay. Thought maybe you hadn't grabbed lunch yet, wanted to see if you were up for some grilled cheese and soup at my place." He laughed. "Came in here looking for you, and I guess I tripped on my own feet or something. Fell right at the thing. Reached out to try to stop myself, but my arm went straight through the glass."

"Oh, I'm so sorry. I went into town. Got groceries and a burrito."

"It's fine. I should have come over earlier."

Kelsea looked at the clock. The pendulum inside the case was smeared with blood that was starting to dry into dark rust-colored streaks.

James must have seen her staring. "Um, sorry about that; I'll pay for it. But just so you know, that old dinosaur hasn't worked in decades, anyway. But you'll still want the glass fixed. I'll take care of it, don't worry. I would put it in my truck today, but I'm not sure I should do any heavy lifting until this closes up a bit." He lifted his arm. The towel was now almost completely red.

"James, that really, *really* looks bad. I should call an ambulance."

"I told you, you can't get through on a cell. And the landline here was disconnected soon after your parents... Well, a while back."

"Then I'll take you."

He laughed, then winced. "Really, I think I'll be fine. It's not as bad as it looks. I just need to keep pressure on it and sit here for a little while."

"Let me get you another towel, at least."

"Sure, thanks. Oh, hey, do you have any juice, or crackers or something? That might be good."

"Sure. I'll be right back."

Kelsea fetched the groceries from the truck and took them into the kitchen. She found a couple of glass tumblers in one of the kitchen cabinets and rinsed the dust off of them. She put them in one of the plastic shopping bags, along with a jug of apple cider and a baguette she had bought, and took it all back to James, stopping by the bathroom on the way for a fresh towel.

James's face showed a little more color on her return, but he still wasn't looking great. She handed him the new towel, then sat down next to him, pulled out the cider, and poured them each a glass.

"Cheers," she said.

"Thanks."

She ripped off pieces of the baguette for them to eat. They ate and drank together in silence for a minute.

"The truck wasn't here," Kelsea said after a while.

"Huh?" James said with a mouth full of bread.

"I mean, didn't you know I was gone? I took the truck with me."

James washed down the bread with few gulps of cider. "Yeah. I guess I just wasn't thinking. Stupid." He smiled sheepishly again.

"No, it's cool. I just thought you were like, this super-intelligent lawyer type, you know?" Kelsea smiled.

James laughed. "Sorry to not live up to the standard." His eyes were bright, and he was starting to look good again.

Real, real *good,* Kelsea thought. The thought caught her by surprise, and she felt her face go red.

"You're really sweet, you know," James said. "It's a shame I didn't get to grow up with you." He paused. "You've become a very beautiful woman."

Kelsea's color deepened. "Well, uh…"

James didn't seem to notice her blushing, or maybe he did and took it as a sign, because he leaned his face close. She didn't have time to think—not that she wanted to—and she met his lips with hers. His scruff against the sides of her mouth felt like sandpaper; it made her shudder in delight. She lifted her hands to his face and held it.

The clock gonged loudly next to them, and they both jerked away from each other in surprise. It kept on, loud, low, and steady.

"I thought you said this thing was broken," Kelsea said above the noise.

"It hasn't rung in years. I would say maybe I fixed it, except if I had, it wouldn't still be going!"

"Well, it can't keep going forever, right? Let's get out of this room until it stops."

She stood and helped James to his feet, though it didn't seem like he needed any help now. He still kept the towel clamped tight against his arm, but not as much blood was soaking through. They escaped to the living room and sat down on the couch. The clock still rang muffled low chimes through the halls, as if making up for all its years of silence.

James looked uncomfortably at her. "Listen," he said. "I'm, uh… I suppose maybe it was the blood loss. I normally don't come on like that. I'm really sorry."

Kelsea felt both disappointed and relieved at the same time. "It's fine. I mean, I'm flattered. And it takes two for—for that. But the truth is, I'm not looking for anything serious right now. Work, and the house, and—"

James cut her off. "Great. Let's just consider it settled."

The clock stopped. Though Kelsea had expected it to cease eventually, the silence seemed to come on suddenly, like someone had pressed *mute* on a stereo in the middle of a heavy metal song.

"That was weird," Kelsea said.

"Yeah." James looked around. His face showed concern. "Listen, I guess I better go." He got up from the couch, still holding his arm. "Again, sorry about everything. I'll see you later, then."

Kelsea got up too. "We're still on for dinner, though, right?"

James smiled and looked a little more relaxed. "Yes. Sure. Definitely. I'll come by around five, then."

"See you then," Kelsea said.

"See you."

Kelsea looked out the tall window as James made tracks back to his truck, further packing down the path that was now forming between the vehicles and the front door.

She rubbed her arms. In all the craziness with the clock and James's cut, she had forgotten how cold it was getting in here again. She checked the thermostat. It was still set at seventy, but the thermometer showed fifty. And she didn't have a clue how to fix it.

She turned around and looked out the window again to see James's truck already leaving. Too late to ask him to look at it. She would see him again this evening, though. Maybe after dinner, he would come inside and look at it. Maybe he would stay longer. Maybe…

Kelsea caught herself thinking about the kiss, and what

it might be like to repeat it in a similar scenario tonight. She shook herself out of it. She had work to do: get this place cleaned and on the market, and then get out of West Virginia. A boyfriend was not part of the plan—not even a handsome, rugged, rich lawyer boyfriend.

She put her coat back on, grabbed the roll of extra-large trash bags she had bought at the grocery store, and ripped one off. She would start cleaning in the room with the grandfather clock.

~

Kelsea filled three trash bags with nothing but destroyed books. Some of them looked old, and might even have been somewhat valuable before their demise. She wondered what had happened to them. If there *was* some animal that had lived in here, she would have expected to find some other evidence in addition to all these ripped pages and spines. But so far, no scratches, no scat, no chewed holes in the walls. She hadn't been through the whole house yet, but certainly she would have seen something by now.

But if there's no mice or anything, she thought as she tied up the bags, *what happened to all these books?*

She still knew very little about her biological parents. Could they have done this? And why hadn't James cleaned all this up before she arrived?

And what about the movement she had seen through the window from the outside? It could have been just her imagination. Or a draft in the house, blowing a curtain flap across the glass or lifting one of these pages into the air. She hadn't seen anything clearly, just movement from the corner of her eye. But this mess of torn paper was weird. It was a puzzle she might never solve.

Another puzzle presented itself to her mind, though, as she swept the glass fragments into a pile. James had said he had fallen *into* the clock. But broken glass was sprayed *outward* across the floor, almost clear to the other wall.

She peered into the clock's pendulum chamber. There wasn't a single piece of glass on the inside.

She noticed something in the corner of the chamber. She reached inside and pulled out a slender brass skeleton key that had been taped to the wood. The bow of the key was ornate and shaped like a crown.

That creepy feeling from last night returned to her as she felt the weight of the key in her palm.

What is this?

She tried to shrug the feeling off, but something just wasn't adding up here.

It's these dark, lonely hills, she thought, pocketing the key. *West Virginia is getting to me, that's all.*

She wondered how her parents had lived so long in this house by themselves, so far even from Davis, which wasn't exactly a metropolitan hub.

CRAZY Hendricks's Place, the sign at the end of the driveway read. Maybe the anonymous vandal's inscription wasn't that far off.

Chapter Five

Kelsea finished cleaning and sorting through all the odds and ends in the room with the clock. She didn't find anything that would shed any light on who her family was, nor did she find anything of value. The furniture, especially the TV and pool table, had value of course, but she would include those in the sale of the house.

She was cleaning the study when she heard a knocking on the front door.

"Coming," she said.

James was here already; she had lost track of time. She smoothed her hair on her way to the living room and hoped she didn't need any makeup.

"Howdy, stranger," James said when she opened the door. He knocked his boots off and stepped inside. "Jeez, what are you, an Eskimo? Here I was thinking of you as some wimpy LA city princess. You could freeze *me* out of here, and that's no joke!"

"Yeah, something's wrong with the heater, I think," Kelsea said. "I was hoping you could look at it. Maybe after dinner?"

"I'll be glad to," James said. "Can't make many promises,

though. I'm a lawyer, remember, not a furnace technician. And it'll be an uphill battle until you get them broken windows replaced." He looked around with his hands in his coat pockets. "Well, I see you already have your coat on. Why don't we head out? You good with pizza?"

"Pizza sounds *great*," Kelsea said.

~

James took her to a small, quirky place in Davis called Sirianni's Cafe. A yeasty, cheesy pizza aroma greeted them when they walked in, warm and safe and unrelenting, like a fat old grandmother's hug. They sat in a tiny booth next to a wooden statue of a Native American chief. A young girl, probably just finishing high school, came over and filled some glasses of water for them.

"Hey there, Jimmy," she said. "Who's the new girl?"

"This here is my friend, Kelsea Stone," James said. "She's from Los Angeles."

The girl's eyes and smile got wider. "Wow, California! Well, welcome to West Virginia," she said. "What should I get you two to drink?"

James looked at Kelsea. "Beer? We've got some good local brews."

"Sure. Sounds great."

James ordered two craft beers. "And we'll get a large Triple X." He looked again at Kelsea. "Wait, you're not a vegetarian or anything, are you?"

Kelsea shook her head. "Whatever a Triple X is, I'll eat it. I'm pretty starving."

The waitress wrote down their order. "All right, I'll be back in a bit with your drinks and the pizza." She hurried away.

"So," Kelsea said. "Jimmy, huh?"

James shrugged. "Folks always called me Jimmy growing up. With clients, I go by James. Sounds more professional. But around here…" He motioned to the room, but Kelsea knew he meant the town. "We're family, you know?"

Kelsea nodded, but in fact she *didn't* know, not really. Even if she lived somewhere smaller than LA, where the masses of people gave her the independence and anonymity she thought she loved, she still wouldn't know anything of family, at least not experientially.

James seemed to realize this and winced. "I'm sorry," he said.

Kelsea shrugged. "It's fine. I get what you mean, though." She sipped on her water. "So, listen. I was wondering. Nobody ever really told me about how… you know. Like, was it cancer? I mean, it's not like they were that old…"

James looked down and stirred the ice cubes in his glass with his straw. "Heart attack, both of them. Really strange. They went together, or one right soon after the other, maybe. I'm actually the one that found them. I would check on them every week, see if they were okay, if they needed me to run to town or anything, you know. Came in, and there they both were, sitting on the sofa next to each other. I knew they were gone before I even checked their pulse. Sometimes you just know."

"Both of them, just like that?"

"Yeah."

"Huh." Kelsea couldn't figure out what else to say. She sipped her water again and stared at the chief's headdress sticking out over the booth behind James, wondering how any average person would feel about hearing this kind of thing. Wondering how she felt herself.

At the back of the restaurant, some kids kept pecking at the jukebox's buttons, watching the album covers flip over behind the glass. At a long table near the register, a loud group of high schoolers was celebrating someone's birthday. Someone yelled something, and they all laughed as they stretched cheesy slices to their plates.

The waitress came by with the food and beers not too long after. The pizza was huge, with at least three inches of cheese, different kinds of meat, olives, and peppers piled on top. James smiled and cut into it. He pulled a slice high off the pan and used his fork to break the gooey cheese strings still clinging to the pie.

"Eat up," he said, and he dished the wedge onto Kelsea's plate.

~

The pizza was gone too fast. Kelsea felt like her stomach was three times the size it was when she came in.

"Holy crap," she said. "That was good."

James leaned back in his chair. "Yeah, best pizza in the world right here." He belched and covered his mouth. "Whoa, sorry."

While James was handing cash to the girl at the register

and making small talk, Kelsea noticed an old man at a table by the door staring at her from under bushy gray eyebrows. His mouth was hidden under a prodigious mustache, and his shirt was stained brown on the collar where it looked like some tobacco juice had dribbled down. Kelsea self-consciously looked away.

James turned to her. "You ready?"

"Yeah."

She tried to ignore the staring redneck as they walked out the door, but she could feel his glare as they passed.

They got to the truck before Kelsea realized she had left her purse in the restaurant. She put her hand to her face. "Hey, sorry," she told James. "I'll be right back."

"No prob. I'll heat it up for us."

She ran back inside and found her purse in the booth. She grabbed it and then tried to speed-walk past the redneck on her way out, but he reached out a thick, dirty hand and grabbed her arm. She looked down at him.

"Careful, girl!" he whispered. There was urgency in his voice and eyes.

Kelsea jerked her arm back in terror. She fumbled for the door, unable in her fear to unlock her eyes from the old man's.

"I said careful! That boy ain't—"

Her hand finally found the handle, and she didn't stick around to hear the rest. She bolted out of the restaurant and ran for the truck, which James had started. She jumped up into the passenger seat, then slammed the door with a sigh.

"Whoa, you all right, there?"

"Yeah. Sorry. Some old creep was ogling me. Freaked me

out a bit." She felt her ears get hot, embarrassed for James to see her ruffled like this. She was glad for the darkness that hid her blush.

"Hey, every town's got 'em," James said. He put the truck in gear and headed back toward Canaan.

~

"Here we are," James said.

Kelsea jolted; she had dozed off on the drive back to the house. She gathered her things.

"Thanks, James," she said.

"Please. Call me Jimmy. I think after that kiss and dinner we should at least drop the formalities."

"Jimmy, huh?" She smiled. She was glad that he seemed comfortable about bringing up the kiss now, but calling him "Jimmy" felt strange, like he was her brother or something. She pictured him as a high school kid, swinging from a rope into a slow-moving river, or whatever kids around here did with their summers when they were young. She laughed.

"What?"

"Nothing. I was just—forget it. I think I'll stick with James, if you don't mind. Sounds more grown up."

"Hey, that's fine, too."

Snow fell lightly as they walked to the front door. The night was dark; the only lights were the ones still illuminating the trails of the nearby ski resort. A far cry from the lights of LA, but she found these comforting, better than the eerie blankness that would darken the valley as soon as the resort shut down for the night.

Kelsea unlocked the door and walked inside. James flipped on the lights and walked to the thermostat.

"Hm," he said. "It's still set. Heat *should* be on."

He disappeared down one of the hallways. Kelsea thought of following him, but instead she just set her purse on the couch and plopped down. She pulled a musty blanket from the back of the couch, wrapped herself in it, and looked up at the deer mounted above the fireplace.

"Don't judge me," she said. "You have fur. And you're dead."

"What?" James popped back into the room.

"Um, nothing," Kelsea said. "I was just, uh, talking to myself. So what's the verdict on the heat?"

James scratched his head. "Well, to be honest, I don't really know much about this stuff. The only thing I can think of is the thermocouple. But that's because I don't know anything else. I could pick one up in town for you tomorrow. Everything's closed now."

Kelsea shuddered. "You mean I've got to live like this until *tomorrow*?"

James laughed. "No. I'll get some firewood from out back. We'll have it roasting in here in no time."

Kelsea smiled. "Sounds great."

James disappeared again, presumably going out the back door to get the wood. Kelsea stood, keeping the blanket wrapped around her, and walked over to the kitchen. She found a kettle and put some water on the stove to boil. In town, she had grabbed some hot chocolate packets from the grocery store as an afterthought, and now she was glad she had. She pulled two mugs off some hooks under the cupboard and poured chocolate powder mix into each.

By the time the water was boiling, she heard James's footsteps coming heavily down the hall. He entered with a canvas bag full of wood slung over one shoulder, wincing a bit. Kelsea had forgotten about that gash on his arm.

"James, I'm sorry. I should have helped. I wasn't thinking."

He set the bag down next to the fireplace and shook his head. "No, don't worry. Not a woman's job."

Kelsea didn't know whether to take offense or feel grateful, so she said nothing. She poured the hot water into the mugs and stirred. "I made us some hot chocolate."

"Great idea. I'll get the fire going before I drink mine."

"Okay." She left his mug on the counter and took hers over to the couch. She sipped the cocoa while James hunched over the fireplace, arranging the logs and stuffing newspaper under and around them. In a couple of minutes he had the fire going strong. He turned off the overhead light so that it was just the light from the fireplace, then he grabbed his cocoa and sat down next to Kelsea.

"I'll come by and take that clock from you tomorrow," James said between sips of his cocoa. "I'll see if I can't find somebody to repair the glass. Real sorry about that."

"No worries. How is your cut?"

James rolled up his sleeve to expose his bandaged forearm. Some red showed through the gauze, but not much. "Not too bad. I think I might have ripped it open a bit while I was getting the firewood, but I think I'll be all right."

"You didn't go to the hospital after you left? James, you probably need stitches!"

He rolled his sleeve back down and gave her a sheepish smile. "Yeah, I reckon maybe I should have. But uh, I just didn't feel like driving all the way to the hospital. So I… well, I had some superglue at the house, so…"

"You did not."

James shrugged. "It worked, mostly." He looked away and slurped more of his hot chocolate.

Kelsea shook her head. "Unbelievable." She scooted closer to him. She watched his face, trying to determine his reaction to her proximity. He just stared into the fire, his blue eyes drinking in the orange flames, his expression intense but impossible to read. His brow tightened, then relaxed, then tightened up again.

"What are you thinking about?" she said.

He looked at her, surprised, as if he had forgotten she was there. "Oh. Nothing. Just old memories."

He stood up suddenly. His eyes darted around the room.

"You okay?" she said.

"It's fine. I just, uh, I just remembered…" He met Kelsea's eyes only for a second, then his gaze shifted back and forth around the room. "I should be going. I'll be back tomorrow with that thermocouple. And I'll take…" He lowered his voice to a whisper, though Kelsea wasn't sure he realized it. "I'll take the clock."

Kelsea nodded. "Okay. Um, well, thanks for dinner. And the fire."

"No problem." James was walking toward the door now,

awkwardly trying to hurry and appear casual at the same time. "Uh, thanks for the hot chocolate. And um, you might want to sleep on the couch tonight. The rest of the house won't get as warm as the living room, and you'll probably need to put a few more logs on there sooner or later."

He opened the front door, and with a short "Goodnight" and his eyes quickly darting back to meet Kelsea's and away once more, like a flame's flickering, he walked out and pulled the door shut behind him.

Kelsea frowned. *What was that about?*

But she couldn't worry about his strange behavior for very long. The room was warm and she was getting drowsy, and her thoughts became soft and slippery. She readjusted the blanket around her shoulders and leaned back into the couch.

Strange shadows danced around the room and reflected in Mr. Deer's glass eyes, making them sparkle with lifelike animation. It was unsettling, the way those eyes seemed to rest on Kelsea with intent—benevolent or malicious, she wasn't sure. But she was still awake enough to know that she couldn't trust her thoughts this late at night, so as she drifted off, she tried to ignore the little girl standing at the loft railing, staring down at her with fire in her eyes like the mounted deer. She told herself it wasn't real, that she was dreaming, and she let her heavy eyelids block out the mind's fabrication as she fell asleep.

~

Kelsea awoke. The fire had gone out, and it was cold even with the blanket. It was still night. She didn't know what the hour was—her phone was in her purse, which was on the floor just out of reach, and she didn't want to leave what little warmth the blanket still provided.

Though the fire was out and all the lights were off, she could see pretty well. She looked out the large windows. The clouds had gone, and in the sky was a moon so bright that Kelsea almost had to squint so it wouldn't hurt her eyes. She turned back and looked at her purse again, the contents of which, she now realized, were spilled out and scattered across the hardwood.

I must have kicked it off the couch while I slept.

The bright blue moonlight showed the puffs of her breath. She reconfigured her blanket to maximize coverage, but it was no use. She was going to have to get the fire going again. Which meant she had to get off the couch.

With the will and burden of Atlas heaving the world on his back, she rose from the couch and shuffled to the fireplace. Fortunately, James had left two extra logs for her to throw on later. She took the iron poker and stirred the ashes. There was still a small bit of heat coming off of them. Would it be enough to catch the logs? Kelsea didn't have any experience with this kind of thing.

She set the logs on the ashes, trying to remember how James had arranged them before. It looked right, but only after a few seconds she knew that "looking right" wasn't going to do the trick. She took some of the newspaper from a basket next to the pokers and stuffed it under one of the logs. It started smoking, and in a few seconds it was brightly flaming underneath. But it started going out before it could catch the wood, so she kept stuffing in more newspaper like mad until she ran out and bits of newspaper ash swirled in the air around her head. Still, it was enough; the logs had caught at last.

Remembering a few movies she had seen, she blew on the glowing ashes, and the fire grew until she was sure it wouldn't go out.

Two logs, though, weren't going to last long. She knew she would need more, but it was all outside. She groaned. If she didn't get it now, she would be even colder later. So she picked up the canvas log carrier and headed down the hall toward the back door.

There wasn't much light in the hall, and the flames had ruined her night vision. She moved slowly, feeling the wall with one hand to guide her, the floor creaking under her step. She finally found the room. In the corner was that broken, bloodstained grandfather clock. She felt like it was watching her as she walked to the glass doors. She unlocked them and worked up the guts she needed to go outside. She regretted not grabbing her coat before heading here, but she didn't feel like going back for it. She just wanted to get this over with. She had fallen asleep in her shoes, so at least she had that.

Now or never.

She opened the doors and stepped out onto the soft snowy deck. The outside air stole her breath, but it also woke her fully. She high-stepped through the knee-deep snow toward the pile of firewood next to the shed, filled the canvas with as many logs as she thought she could carry, then followed her foot-holes back inside. She shut the door behind her and shivered. She had worked up some sweat despite the temperature, and now that sweat chilled her. She wiped her sleeve across her forehead.

As she started back across the room, she heard a ticking sound. She looked over at the grandfather clock and saw the bloody pendulum swinging back and forth, reflecting the blue midnight light let in through the French doors.

Kelsea walked over to the clock and peered at it. The hands began to move around the face, getting progressively faster, and then the clock started to chime. Kelsea backed away, picked up the bag of wood, and ran back down the hall to the living room. She didn't know why it scared her so much—it was just a broken clock, after all—but she was relieved when the chiming stopped again, abruptly as before, and the only sound that was left was the crackling fire.

After stuffing a few more logs into the fireplace, she lay back down on the couch, this time taking off her shoes. Soon the fire had gone from a crackle to a roar, and she was getting hot with the blanket on. She kicked it off and looked out the window. The fire was reflected in the glass, superimposed over the snow-covered trees outside.

She couldn't remember ever seeing the moon like this in all her many nights out in LA. Surely it had been there—she knew the moon was always *there*—but she was just so distracted by the lights of the city that she forgot about the light up there in the sky.

She missed the city lights, but she had to admit that the moon had its own appeal.

Something else reflected in the glass—a flash of movement she couldn't identify. She turned over and sat up. A shadow moved in the hall.

This was it. The animal. It was time. It was her *destiny*.

"You're *so* going down," she muttered.

She got up and stepped into the hall just in time to see the shadow escape up the stairway. She tried to move as quickly and soundlessly as possible. The floor was cold and slippery under her socked feet. When she got to the foot of the stairway, she heard a board creak at the top.

It was only then that she wondered what she was even going to do if she was able to corner the animal. She had no weapon, no net, nothing she could subdue it with. What if it was rabid? And while it was impossible to make out any detail, that shadow had seemed a lot larger than any animal she had been expecting. What if it could hurt her?

She ran back to the fireplace and grabbed one of the fire irons. It was heavy and warm from being next to the fire. *This should do the trick.*

Out of the corner of her eye, she saw something reflected in the window again. She looked fully at the reflection. Something ran past the railing in the loft. No, not some*thing*.

She blinked. *A girl?*

And then it was gone.

She had to have imagined it. It was a trick of the moon, the trees, the snow—her sleep-deprived mind had filled in the image of a little girl where the animal had been.

Still, it gave her pause. She was no longer so gung-ho about hunting this creature down. Maybe she could share the house one more night. It hadn't been bothering her, after all. And with her mind in this state, was it really a good idea to go running around this old house in the middle of the night, swinging an iron rod around?

Her eyes still locked on the loft's reflection in the window—no girl, though, and no animal either—she lowered the iron back down to the rack. A bit dazed, and not at all confident about her decision, she collapsed back onto the couch, pulled the blanket back over herself, and closed her eyes, trying desperately not to think about little girls or giant rabid raccoons.

Chapter Six

It was morning, and cold again. Kelsea rubbed her eyes and looked around. Her phone was still on the floor, but judging by the light, it was probably seven or eight. The fire was out, of course. She needed to get up and put some more wood on it, but instead she buried herself under the blanket for fifteen more minutes.

She finally got off the couch and put some more logs on the fire. But blowing on the coals wasn't enough to get it going again, and she was out of newspaper. She wrapped her blanket over her shoulders and sat there on the rug pitying herself for a few minutes before she remembered all the ruined books she had bagged up. She went into the office, dragged one of the trash bags of paper back to the fireplace, and pulled out a handful of yellowed pages. They caught quickly on the coals, and a torn-up copy of *Moby Dick* soon got the fire going again.

Kelsea then took a *very* short shower. Apparently the hot water was connected to the central heating, so the water was ice cold. She put on her clothes as fast as she ever had in her life and rushed back into the warm living room after setting some water on the stove to boil for hot chocolate.

She sat close to the fire. Soon the kettle was screaming. She poured herself some hot chocolate and considered her options from the couch. She could clean now, while the rest of the house was still an icebox. Or she could stay here in front of the fire until James returned to fix the furnace.

An easy decision.

She pulled her laptop from her luggage and sat with a blanket around her knees while she worked on her article.

~

A noise broke her concentration—a creaking sound from down the hall. The house settling? Or her unwelcome houseguest?

She took the fireplace poker in her hand like she had last night and snuck down the hall. The sound came again, from directly above her. She climbed the stair.

At the top, she looked both ways. A door moved slightly. Still in her socks, she slid her feet silently across the floor until she reached it. Whatever this thing was, she had it cornered now.

She flung the door open and stepped inside the room, holding the poker high, ready to strike down whatever unfortunate creature was destined to suffer her wrath.

The room was a child's bedroom. Two small beds with pink blankets were against a wall. Soft yellow stars and lavender horses danced across the wallpaper all around her. A large, elaborate dollhouse was on the other side of the room. In her mind, Kelsea saw herself as a child, kneeling here on the floor, playing with the dolls, speaking different voices for each wooden character. The scene came to her with force and vividness, almost as if her past self had appeared there in front of her own eyes. It took her by surprise.

This had been *her* room, once.

She sat down on one of the beds, and dust rose around her. Her parents must not have touched this place since they got rid of her. She still couldn't wrap her head around why they would have put her up for adoption. If she had so cramped their style, why had they kept all these toys and kid decorations? Something just wasn't adding up.

The lace bedskirt hanging from the other small bed moved as if it had just been touched. *The animal.* She reached the poker toward the lace to lift it up—

"Kelsea?" James's voice came from downstairs, and Kelsea jerked, dropping the poker.

"Yeah. I'm up here."

She picked up the poker, eyed the lace for a second, then backed away. As long as James was here, she may as well wait for him to come up before taking on a rabid raccoon.

When she heard James come up the stairs, she stuck her head out the door. "In here, quick," she whispered.

James came in, and she quietly pointed the poker at the bed. The skirt was moving again.

"What is it?" James asked.

"Look. There's this animal. I think it's been living in the house. I finally cornered it. It's under the bed right there."

"What kind of animal?"

"I don't know. I haven't gotten a good look at it. It's pretty big, whatever it is."

James took a step toward the bed, then froze. "You sure you aren't imagining something?"

"Yes I'm sure! I've heard this thing creeping around. I've *seen* it!"

"I thought you said you haven't seen it."

"Well, not *really*, but I mean, I've seen glimpses. I mean, look, there's something under there."

James's face paled, turning almost as gray as it had yesterday after he had cut his arm.

"What?" Kelsea whispered. "What's wrong with you?"

"Nothing." He grabbed her elbow and tugged at her. "Come on, I think we should go."

She jerked her elbow away. "What's with you? There's a freaking *animal* living in my *house*. I want to get rid of it! What, are you scared?"

"No, I'm just… I think it's your imagination. There's no animal living here; we would have found a nest or droppings or something by now. This place is clean. Listen, I just came over to install this thermocouple and pick up the broken clock." He turned and left the room.

Kelsea stood there looking at the empty doorway, at a loss to explain James's behavior. If he really didn't think there was something under the bed, he would have walked right up to it and proven her wrong—wouldn't he? Something had him freaked out. And while Kelsea couldn't say that she really wanted to go face to face with a badger or giant rat or whatever was under the bed, she wouldn't have expected that response from James. Maybe he had a phobia or something.

It's up to you, Kels. Gotta do what you gotta do.

Kelsea crept toward the bed, hesitantly. She took a breath to steady her nerves, leaned down, then lifted the skirt, ready to strike with her fire poker.

There was nothing under there but a bunch of little girls' shoes. Whatever had been there must have snuck out while her back was turned.

Sighing, and frankly a bit relieved that nothing had been there to claw her face off, she withdrew from the bedroom. On her way down the stairwell, she heard the heat kick on.

She replaced the fire poker to its stand next to the fireplace. James walked into the living room, smiling, all traces of his unexplained terror gone. He wiped his hands together.

"Easy peasy. Got the heat going again. I was afraid it would be more complicated than that, but looks like we're okay."

"Thanks."

"Don't mention it. You want me to get that grandfather clock now? I don't know where I'll get it fixed, but I'm sure I can find someone for you. In fact, if it can't get fixed until after this week, we could get your key copied and I could just bring it back myself. You wouldn't have to worry about anything. If you're okay with that."

"Yeah, sure, whatever we need to do. You've already been through the place before I even knew about it, anyway. Oh, hey, that reminds me. You said you went through and cleaned and took care of the place before I got here, right?"

"Yeah, why?"

"Well, I guess it has to do with this animal thing. When I got here, there were books all torn up and thrown around a couple of the rooms. You saw the mess in the room with the clock. I'm assuming it wasn't like that when you cleaned?"

"No, it wasn't."

"Well, then that settles it, right? I'm not imagining things here. There's something else living in this house."

James looked away. "Yes," he said. "Something else is living here." He looked back at her with an expression she couldn't read. "I'll try to take care of it. I'll, uh, contact an exterminator today. Maybe we can get an appointment before you leave. If not, I'd be glad to make sure he comes over sometime after."

"Okay, thanks. I guess if that's the best we can do."

"Well, I'm going to run out to the truck and get my dolly, then I might need your help moving that clock out." He shrugged. "Sore arm and all. Sorry."

"Yeah, no, it's fine. Sure."

James wheeled his dolly to the grandfather clock. He removed the clock's pendulums and weights and set them aside, then had Kelsea hold the dolly still while he shuffled it onto the base. Once they had it on, he strapped it in tight and took it outside to the pickup. He had backed his truck right up to the front steps so they wouldn't have to drag the dolly through the snow.

"Now comes the fun part," James said. "I don't have a ramp or anything. So if you get up on the bed and hold this from the handle, I'll lift from the bottom and set it up on the tailgate."

Kelsea did as he instructed. Even though James still seemed to favor his cut arm, he squatted down and lifted the loaded dolly onto the truck with relative ease. They lowered the clock onto its back against some cardboard that was spread out on the truck bed.

Kelsea took in the view of the woods surrounding the house while James strapped the clock down. The sky was still clear, and the sun was reflecting brightly off of the snow.

She saw something moving through the trees. She squinted and put a hand to her eyes to shield them from the light. There was some movement, some rustling branches, and then the figure disappeared, hidden by the forest and the glare.

"That should do it," James said. "What are you looking at?"

"Nothing. I just thought I saw something in the woods."

"Probably a deer. They're all over the place."

"Yeah. Just weird, right? I mean, all these animals could be watching us and we wouldn't even know it."

James shrugged. "They ain't gonna hurt you. They're just animals."

Kelsea nodded, a little embarrassed. "Yeah, I guess."

"Anyways, I'm going to head out. Stuff to do at the house, and I'll try and see what I can find out about getting this clock fixed."

"And the exterminator."

"Right. And that."

They stepped off the truck onto the deck. They stood looking at each other for an awkward second.

"Thanks for fixing the heater," Kelsea said.

"Yeah, no problem. I, uh… I'll see you later." He turned and walked to the driver's side of the cab. "Hey, I—do you want to do dinner again tonight?"

Kelsea smiled. "Sure, sounds great."

"Pick you up at five?"

"Sure."

"Great. See you then."

James grinned and got in the truck. The engine rumbled to life, and Kelsea watched him drive away before turning to go back inside.

Just dinner, Kelsea thought. *Nothing serious. Might as well make the best of my time while I'm here.*

As she was about to open the door, movement flashed in the corner of her eye. She turned and looked back into the woods. There was definitely something moving, and it didn't look like a deer.

Is that a girl?

"Hello?" Kelsea called. "Hello, is someone out there?"

The child started running around the inside edge of the woods toward the back yard. Kelsea ran off of the deck and headed for the trees. She was amazed at how fast the child ran through the snow: it barely slowed, while Kelsea felt like she was in one of those nightmares where her legs would only move in slow motion. By the time Kelsea reached the woods, the kid was already far ahead of her.

The snow wasn't as deep in the woods though, and Kelsea was able to move more quickly. She was starting to close the gap when the child left the cover of the trees and ran straight through the yard toward the shed.

The girl—it was definitely a girl, and she looked to be not much older than five or six, but how she *ran!*—entered the shed, and the door swung shut behind her.

Kelsea huffed and puffed to the shed. She opened the door. A musty scent of rotten wood, old grass clippings, and gasoline confronted her. She could see a rusty lawnmower and some shelves full of tools and other odds and ends, but most of the shed's interior was hidden in black shadow. She didn't see the girl; she must be against the back wall, hiding in the darkness.

"Hello? I'm not going to hurt you." Kelsea stepped forward slowly. The old plywood floor bent under her foot. "I want to help you."

Wind blew the door shut behind Kelsea. She screamed in surprise, and the darkness covered her. She pushed back on the door, but it was latched shut. Without any light, she couldn't figure out how to open the door from the inside. As she felt along the wall for a light switch and found none, she struggled to hold down her rising panic. It was dark and cold, but if she could keep her head, she would get the door open eventually. Besides, the girl was probably as scared Kelsea was, if not more, and she didn't want to do anything that would make that worse.

"It's all right. We'll get out of this," she said to the girl, whom she still could neither see nor hear. *She must be terrified,* Kelsea thought. *She's totally silent—I wonder if she's holding her breath.*

Kelsea felt a string across her face, and thinking it was a spider's web, swatted furiously at it. It swung back and forth against her with more weight than a web, though, and Kelsea realized it was a light cord. Her hands found it in the dark, and she tugged on it lightly. A single incandescent bulb painted the shed's interior with yellow light and long shadows.

"There now, we can finally—"

She stopped. The girl wasn't in the back of the shed. She wasn't in the shed at all.

What the hell?

She looked around. In the light now, she noticed a bunch of wooden chains hanging from the rafters, each carved from a single piece of wood, it appeared. She considered them for a moment, wondering if her father had made them, and how he might have carved the links out of one piece.

She could think about that later. Right now she had to find that girl. She stepped carefully around the mower toward the back of the shed. There was a shadowy spot below a shelf in the corner; the girl might be curled up there. Kelsea stooped down and looked into the dark space.

No girl. Just a large green box.

Kelsea felt a significance to the box that she could not explain. She pushed the mower away to make some space on the dusty floor and dragged the box out, her curiosity overriding both her bewilderment about the missing girl and the predicament of being trapped inside this cold shed.

The box was about four feet long, and a couple feet wide and deep. It was made of green-painted wood, with a hinged lid and a brass keyhole. She tried to pry the lid open with her fingers, but she couldn't get enough purchase. She rustled around the shelves and found a long flathead screwdriver. She jammed that under the lid and bore down. The screwdriver bowed slightly under her weight, but the lid didn't surrender.

She rubbed her arms and held them tight to her sides. She could come back to the box later; right now, she needed to get out of here.

With the light on, now she could see clearly the lever that would open the door. She stood to leave, then paused. Maybe she should bring the box with her. She felt a strange attraction to it. It was more than just curiosity; it was almost a magnetic or mystical force—not that she believed in that sort of thing. She felt as though she needed to protect whatever was in it.

But she shook that feeling off. There was no logical reason to take it inside with her. And besides, she wasn't sure if she could even carry it in by herself.

She walked to the door. That box had somehow erased the girl from her mind, and now she felt embarrassed that she had been so easily distracted. Where had the girl gone? Maybe the girl had somehow snuck past her and squeezed out the doorway before the door was blown shut. Maybe it wasn't the wind that had slammed the door shut after all— maybe the girl had been hiding next to the door, and when

Kelsea stepped further in, the girl slipped out and shut Kelsea inside. But why?

It was far too cold for a girl that young to be out here by herself, and she hadn't even been dressed properly. Though Kelsea hadn't gotten a good look at her face, she had seen that the girl was without hat or coat, wearing only a yellow summer dress, and barefoot, even. Kelsea had to find this girl soon and get her back to her parents, or she would freeze.

She opened the door to the blinding sun and snow. She put her arm up to her face and looked around for footprints in the snow. She found none but her own. She remembered how the girl had looked like she was running across the snow's surface, without sinking—but that couldn't have been. The snow didn't even have a layer of crusty ice over it; even a girl that young would have made tracks. Kelsea must have covered the girl's tracks with her own, and then the girl could have followed them back into the woods without leaving a new trail.

Kelsea ran back into the woods, looking for some sign of the girl. All she could find was her own trail from before.

She ran back inside and found her cell phone. No service.

She had to call somebody. James, the police, search and rescue, *anyone*—she had to find this girl.

She copied her house address to a scrap of paper, put it with her phone in her purse, ran to the truck, and started driving to town. Dark black clouds were blowing in over the mountains behind her, bringing with them a sense of helplessness and dread.

Her eyes darted back and forth from the road to her

phone, waiting for some service. She finally found a couple bars just before entering Davis. In her excitement, she pulled over a little too quickly, and the truck fishtailed then slid off the road into a soft snow bank.

After she got over the shock of driving off the road, she took stock of herself and the truck and realized that nothing had really been damaged. She caught her breath and dialed 911.

~

Cooper could hardly believe it. A pre-war Martin D-28 guitar, vintage 1936. Brazilian rosewood back. Original nickel-plated Grover tuners. Mint condition, or close, from what he could tell from the pictures. Only about sixty of these were ever *made*, and some idiot on the Virginia coast had it listed for ten thousand bucks. Clearly this guy didn't know what he was selling.

As soon as Cooper came across it on Craigslist, he had taken the next few days off to make the trip to Norfolk. He wasn't going to risk having it get snatched up by someone else. He would know if it was worth it once he got there and inspected it himself. If it wasn't the real deal, he would only be out for the gas and hotel, and at least he would get a day or two in some relatively warm weather. And if this was legitimate, it would be a steal.

Ten thousand dollars, Coop thought, still unbelieving. His head swam as he stuffed an extra change of clothes in his bag and zipped it up. *Can this be real?*

It could be a trick, sure, or a scam. But he would never

forgive himself if he didn't go see it with his own eyes.

"You got everything ready, dear?" his wife called from the kitchen.

"Yup." He threw the bag over his shoulder and went to kiss his wife goodbye.

"I made you a PBJ for the road," she said. "How much did you say he's selling it for?"

"Oh…" he said. "Not much, trust me." His wife tolerated, but did not share, his passion for collectable bluegrass instruments, and even though ten grand was nothing for such a specimen as this, it was still ten grand, and he thought it best to stay vague on the details.

"And how much is it worth?"

"If it's what I think it is, could be more than a hundred grand."

Even his wife was staggered by the prospect. "Wow," she said. She eyed him for a moment, as if considering whether she wanted to know how much of his paycheck he was about to part with. Apparently she agreed it was in the best interests of their marriage for her to stay in the dark, as all she said was, "How long will you be gone, again?"

"A couple nights. You know how I am after long drives. But that's all. You'll hardly miss me." He gave her a peck on the cheek.

"Take the Subaru," she said. "Better than that gas-guzzling truck of yours."

"You got it."

He was just backing out of the driveway when his wife came running out of the house, waving. "You have a call," she said. "It's from the station."

He left the vehicle idling and went back inside to answer the phone. "This is Coop."

"Hey, Sheriff, it's Rose. Listen, I know you aren't coming in today, but this call just came in, and Ralph really has his hands full at the moment with a domestic disturbance in St. George."

"I'm about to go out of town, Rose."

"I know, I'm sorry. But this lady sounded pretty frantic. Signal kept fading in and out. I caught the address, but I'm not so sure about what's going on. It's in Canaan. I thought since you lived past Hambleton that way, maybe you could check it out real quick?"

Coop sighed. *If I had just left earlier this morning, like I meant to…*

He supposed he *could* swing around through Canaan on his way. It would add about twenty minutes, but Rose was right that he could get there more quickly, especially if Ralph was the same distance the other way.

"All right. I'll check it out on my way. If it's important, I'll call you. It's probably just some out-of-towner freaking out about… I don't know. You know how they get."

"Uh-huh. Well, thanks, Sheriff. Again, really sorry to bother you."

"It's no problem. See you later."

"Later."

~

The dispatcher had said the police were on their way to the house, which was great, except now *Kelsea* couldn't get to the house. Even in four-wheel drive, she couldn't get the tires to do anything but spin, digging her deeper into the snow. She tried calling James, but her calls went straight to voicemail.

"Come *on*!" She slammed her hand against the steering wheel. *I'm not going to cry. I'm not going to cry.*

An old wood-paneled Jeep Grand Cherokee stopped on the road in front of her. The driver got out and walked up to her door. It took her a moment to recognize him; it was the old redneck who had been spying on her at the pizza place the night before. The old creep was still wearing the exact same tobacco-stained shirt, too. She locked her doors.

He knocked on her window. She didn't roll it down. "You in some trouble, miss?" he said through the glass.

She shook her head. "No, I'm fine. I can get out myself." She tried the gas again, but the tires just whirred and kicked up slush.

The old man smirked. "I can tell. Listen, you ain't gotta even get out of the truck. I'll shovel you a path. Now just hold yer taters."

He retrieved a short snow shovel from his Jeep and started shoveling the snow behind her tires. Kelsea stayed in her car, still nervous but also feeling sorry for acting so cold to him. When he finished shoveling, he retrieved a bag of cat litter from his vehicle and poured some behind her tires. He came back to Kelsea's window, and this time she lowered it halfway.

"There, now. You got her in four?"

Kelsea checked, then nodded.

"Good. Now just reverse straight back, but don't gun it, all right? You wanna get a good grip on the gravel, not bury 'em back into the snow."

Kelsea backed up while the man watched the road for cars and motioned her out. "You got her, you got her, keep a-comin," he said. "Turn your wheels a mite—straight back now, there you got it."

She made it back onto the road, and he walked to her window again, which she rolled down all the way now. "Looks like we got her," he said.

"Yeah, thanks for the help," she said. "Listen, I'm sorry if I was a little rude."

"Don't mention it. I reckon I did spook you last night. But listen." He looked around, as if there could possibly be anyone around to eavesdrop. "That Jimmy... I don't mean to stick my nose in your business. I'm just sayin—somethin don't sit straight with me about him. I don't trust him."

"Why are you telling me this? You don't even know me."

The man gave her a brown, crooked-toothed smile and jammed his hand through her open window. "Name's Russ. Russ Pifer."

"Kelsea Stone." They shook.

"Well now we know each other. Say, I'd hang around and chat some more, but I gotta scoot. You see that road right behind ya?" He pointed, and Kelsea looked over her shoulder. A narrow road ran off of the main stretch. A green sign poked up through a snow bank reading *CANAAN HEIGHTS RD.* "I live up at the top of the hill. You need anythin, you just give me a holler, okay?"

"Yeah, sure," Kelsea said. She didn't feel quite as scared of this guy now, but she still found it pretty weird that he was telling her where he lived.

"Have a nice day, Miss Stone. And watch out for that Jimmy character. I ain't never trusted him much."

Kelsea waited for him to drive away before she turned around and headed back to the house, toward a sky that was becoming increasingly dark.

Chapter Seven

Kelsea waited inside while the sheriff searched the woods for the girl. The man had showed up without a uniform, without even a patrol vehicle. At first, she hadn't been sure he was a police officer, but he had shown her his badge, and he acted official enough. Still, he didn't seem to know much about what she had told the dispatcher. In fact, if Kelsea had been reading him right, he didn't even believe she had seen the girl in the woods. She felt like he was just humoring her, and she wondered why they hadn't taken her call more seriously. They should have sent a full-fledged search team with medical assistance. But he was here at least, and he had been kind enough to grab a couple of walkie-talkies from his car and leave one with her, so she could call him back if she saw the girl near the house again.

Since she needed to keep an eye on the back yard, she couldn't do much cleaning, so she took her laptop into the clock room (she still thought of it as "the clock room," even now that it was sans clock) and plopped onto a couch to work on her article for *Ensemble*. Every few minutes she would look up and peer out the glass doors to see if the girl had run through the yard and left footprints. The snow was coming down heavily, though, and she had trouble even seeing the shed. If the girl was still out in this, Kelsea had a hard time believing the sheriff would find her alive.

The heater had caught up with the weather and was making up for lost time. Twice Kelsea found herself jolting awake from unintentional catnaps, and soon she was really out.

~

Coop strained his eyes, trying to see any disturbance in the brush and branches. Visibility was terrible and getting worse, even with the forest's mitigating effects on the blowing snow.

This wasn't his first time scouring these woods for a little girl.

He had experienced a cold shudder when Kelsea had described the missing girl to him. *It's her,* he couldn't help thinking. But he had repressed that voice in his head. He didn't believe in such old wives' crock. Dead was dead. It was a coincidence; there were plenty of young girls that would match the same description, and Kelsea hadn't gotten a good look at this one anyway, if indeed she had seen anything at all—which Cooper doubted.

Kelsea didn't acknowledge the coincidence, either. In fact, she didn't even seem to recognize Coop at all. He had been a lot younger back then, fresh and bright-eyed, the youngest officer on the force, ready to take on the world, if not just the county. And she had been a little kid. How long had that been—twenty, thirty years? Well, she sure had grown up since then, and into quite a looker. If he hadn't married…

He saw movement through the trees, and froze. But it was only a deer.

False alarm, he thought. *Just like this whole crazy search.*

He hadn't wanted to go out into the woods, and he had tried to explain to Kelsea how there was no way a little girl without shoes on could have even made it to the property on her own. It's not like there were any next-door neighbors. But Kelsea was adamant that she had seen something, so he decided he could spend fifteen minutes and make a quick loop around the property to satisfy the nervous woman.

He decided to pick up the pace. The storm was getting worse, and he wanted to get on the road before it got too bad. He would make it to the river, follow it for a few minutes, then return to the house.

Yet as he jogged, a sickening feeling crept over him. His heart was beating fast—much faster than could be accounted for by his pace alone. *The girl, the river—no, it isn't that, it can't be.*

Coop's nerves wore thinner with every heavy footfall through the thickening snow. The wind blew sharp crystals into his face, stinging like hundreds of white bees and pasting his eyelashes together when he squinted. He had driven through some bad weather in his life, but this was by far the worst he had ever experienced on foot. It was almost as if the wind was coming from all around, blowing against his face no matter which direction he turned his head. And there was something else, a strange feeling, something unnatural and inexplicable that filled his belly with dread.

He stopped to regain his bearings, turning in a slow circle. He thought he should have reached the creek by now, but all he saw through the storm were trees and brush in every direction.

He heard something to his right and turned; a low pine branch rocked back and forth, raining down sparkling powder. An animal must have brushed against it. He squinted past the tree and caught a glimpse of something small and yellow, not an animal at all, but a—

The lost girl.

Kelsea hadn't imagined it, then. *Shit. I could be here all day. There goes my Martin.*

"Hey, wait!" he called. He took off after the girl, though she was no longer in sight.

How is she moving so fast? I'm no spring chicken, but this is crazy. She should be frostbitten and hypothermic by now.

He broke through some trees, and there was the river. He breathed a sigh of relief. The girl was gone, but at least he had a reference point. And she couldn't have gone too far.

He lifted the radio to his face. "Hey, Kelsea, I think I found her. Don't know how, but she seems fine. Guess she's scared of me, she keeps running away. I can hardly keep up. You there? Over."

He saw a flash of yellow. The little girl was now running through the woods on the other side of the creek.

Radio still in hand, he walked toward the river. If the girl had gotten across, that probably meant that most of the river was frozen, but he was a lot bigger and couldn't take the chance. He started for some boulders he might be able to hop across instead.

Before he made it to the first one, his right foot dropped down, and his boot filled with water, burning and then numbing his foot before he scrambled back to solid ground. He sat there on the bank, gritting his teeth against the pain of his blood coming back into his foot. He banged his boot on the ground a few times to work out the last bit of pins and needles, then stood cautiously.

He should probably tell Kelsea to call the station, let them know to send help. But when he reached to his belt for his radio, he found nothing but hip. He remembered that he had been holding it when he stepped into the water; he must have dropped it when he fell back. He looked around for it, but didn't see it.

He again looked out at the half-frozen creek, and gasped. The girl was standing there, right in the middle. Somehow she was on top of the snow, not even sinking to the tops of her feet, which were bare and pale. But that wasn't the only thing that gave him pause, that caused him to doubt his sanity.

"It can't be," he said. He rubbed the ice crystals from his eyes, shook his head, and peered through the storm. "It can't be *you*. You're…"

The girl in the yellow dress frowned, then opened her mouth as if she were screaming, but all he heard was the wind roaring through the trees.

You're seeing things, Coop. You're cold and scared and your brain isn't firing right.

The girl lowered her shoulders and charged him like a bear.

"It's not real," he said. He squeezed his eyes shut just as the girl came upon him.

Nothing happened. He opened his eyes again. The storm still raged, but there was no girl. He released the air that was trapped in his lungs.

"Wow, Coop, you're really losing—"

Then he felt tiny icicle hands against his back, pushing him forward with impossible strength.

~

Kelsea woke to static on the walkie-talkie and a long line of gibberish on her computer screen from where her hands had fallen upon the keys as she slept. She deleted the unintended text, saved the article, and closed her laptop before she could do any more damage. Outside, the blizzard still painted the glass doors white, though the downfall seemed to have let up a bit since she had fallen asleep.

She picked up the radio and pressed the PTT button. "Hello, Sheriff? Any progress? I dozed off for a while." She released her finger from the button. Then, as an afterthought, she pressed it again and said, "Over."

Nothing but static on the other end. Perhaps he had found the girl and had already taken her to the hospital. She walked to the living room and looked out the front windows. Through the blowing snow she could see the sheriff's Subaru, snow drifted against it up to the side mirrors. He was still out in the woods, and he wasn't answering her calls. Maybe there were problems with the radio. Could the blizzard affect the signal?

Kelsea checked the time on her phone.

Three thirty? I couldn't have slept that long.

She unconsciously chewed her pinky nail while she tried to figure out what had happened.

Everything's probably fine, she thought, trying to fight off the helpless, trapped feeling weighing on her. *He must have found the girl. He found her just before I woke up, and he's on his way back with her now. Maybe he's carrying her, and his hands aren't free to answer the radio. Or maybe the snow ruined the radio somehow.*

She needed to occupy herself somehow to keep from worrying so much. She was almost done with her article anyway; she might as well finish it up. If he wasn't back when she was done, she would try calling James again.

Back in the clock room, she opened her laptop. Her document was still on the screen, but after the last line she had written, there was a new paragraph:

kelsea hendricks turned to Stone
your lust for Him provokes my bones
eyes bright full lips hips sensual
you smile as if death cannot come to you too
death is cold but it is not so bad when you can avenge it

Kelsea put her hand to her mouth. She tried to convince herself that she had written this in some state between wakefulness and sleep, like a writer's version of sleep talking—but this didn't look like it was written *by* her, but *to* her. She couldn't believe there was anything this dark lurking in the murky waters of her subconscious—she was a writer for *Ensemble Weekly,* for crying out loud! She wrote about celebrity hairstyles and hookups and Oscar predictions, not provoked bones and death and avenging.

But if she hadn't written this, then she wasn't alone in this house. And her roommate wasn't just a raccoon coming in from the cold.

Her breathing became shallow, and tears leaked from her eyes. She fought back a scream.

She snapped her laptop shut and stood, fists clenched at her sides. Whoever was here—could they see her right now? Were they watching her? Cold beads of sweat formed at the base of her neck. She looked at her phone.

Of course there's no damn service, she thought. She tried calling James anyway, shaking the phone as if she could bully the call into going through, but it wouldn't connect.

She paced violently back and forth. She was about to hyperventilate. She had to calm down.

She had to *do* something.

She picked up the radio again. "Hello? Sheriff Cooper?"

Nothing but static.

It wasn't safe here. Someone else was in this house, someone sick and demented, someone who knew her name and might have eyes on her at this very moment.

Kelsea looked out the glass doors into the yard drifted deep with snow and the lumpy white-coated trees. The intruder was in the house with her, and the only person who could help her was out there in the woods, not responding to her calls.

I might be safer out in the snow, she thought. It made as much sense to her as anything else, though in the back of her mind she realized she might not be in the most rational state.

She put on her shoes and coat; then she ran out the door into the white and gray.

Chapter Eight

The snow was up to her waist, and only halfway through the yard she was already sweating heavily under her light coat. The wind was loud and proud, and she had to lean against it as she plowed her way through.

As she passed the old shed, she found herself turning her eyes away from it, though she couldn't say why. She thought about that green wooden box stowed in the shadows. And for no reason that she could fathom, she thought about her childhood bedroom, and the dollhouse, and the beds.

Why are there two beds? The thought flew through her head, gone as quickly as it had come, fear and survival instinct pushing it to the back.

The shed was behind her now; the forest wasn't far. Once she made it under the trees the snow wouldn't be nearly as thick, and she could find the sheriff.

She stumbled, fell forward into the snow, and struggled to get back to her feet. She turned to see if anyone was following her, but all she saw was the tall brown triangle of the front of the house poking up behind its rectangular back, and the rickety shed standing in dark contrast to the whiteness that seemed to snatch all hope and breath from her. The tire and rope swung from the apple tree's gnarled hand.

One last frantic push through and she fell into the forest, panting. She looked around as she caught her breath. The trees kept the snow from getting as deep, and she could move a little more freely here. But the impulsiveness that had sent her charging out into the deep snow had faded, along with her strength. Now that she was here, she was reluctant to just run off through the woods mindlessly and get lost.

"Sheriff?" she called. Though she yelled with all the strength she still had, she could hardly hear herself in the wind and muting snow.

She took another look over her shoulder at the house and her trail through the yard. Again, though it was in her field of vision, she avoided focusing on the shed. She turned back to the forest. Tall feathery conifers and leafless hardwoods almost overwhelmed her. Any trail the sheriff might have made had been erased by the storm. Which way would he have taken?

She zipped up her coat a few more inches. She couldn't just stand here for very long. She started off into the woods at a brisk walk.

She kept calling as she went, but she neither heard nor saw any sign of the sheriff's passing. After a while she spotted what looked like a break in the trees up ahead, and she ran to it. The land started to descend, and she heard the trickling of water.

She pushed through a thicket of rhododendron and

found a wide creek. She carefully approached the bank where there was a low spot in the snow; she could see water rushing under a thin layer of ice. Upstream were snow-capped black boulders, water cutting through the frozen crust around them in some places, the covered ice disguising the river as solid ground in others.

Next to one of the boulders the snow dipped in a strange way near the bank, and she walked toward it, careful to watch her footing and not step onto thin ice accidentally. She noticed a gray rectangular object in the snow, and she bent down and picked it up.

It was a radio.

She ran to the dip in the snow, still minding the hidden stream the best she could. A large hole in the ice exposed the water rushing under. An animal must have broken through the ice.

She saw something dark in the river. She leaned forward to see underneath the crust and almost fell in when she saw what it was: a large black boot.

And connected to the boot was a body stuffed up under the ice, entrapped on a submerged rock.

It was the sheriff.

Kelsea backed away from the river and fell onto her butt on the powdery bank. Tears burned in the corners of her eyes, and she brushed them away with the cold wet sleeve of her coat. She got to her feet and ran back the way she had come.

She broke through the trees and barreled through the yard. Her progress was much easier now that she had already created the path, but she still tripped and fell over the holes and packed hills she had left behind. She took the steps two at a time, threw open the French doors, and fell inside. A gust blew fresh snow in after her, and she pushed the doors closed from where she lay on the floor.

Her heart was a steam train full tilt. She stayed there on the floor and tried to regain some clarity.

She knew she wasn't safe in the house, if there was still some perv hiding here. *But at least I'm warm,* she thought. And the simple fact was that she didn't feel safe either in the house or in the woods. *And there aren't any dead bodies in here.*

Not yet, anyway.

She would get out of here, that's what she would do. The roads might be slippery, but James's house wasn't that far away. If she could get out of her driveway, she could probably make it there in one piece.

She had just gotten to her feet when a knocking sounded from the front door. She brushed the melting snow out of her hair and ran to the living room. Through the window in the door she saw that it was that old codger, Russ. Hair bristled on the back of her neck. She secured the lock before speaking to him through the glass.

"What are you doing here?" she said.

"Pardon, I ain't meanin to impose or nothin. I seen the way the storm was actin up and thought I'd come down and check on ya. Everythin okay?"

Part of her wanted to let him inside, to tell him she wasn't all right, that there was a girl lost in the woods, a drowned police officer in the river out back—God knew what had happened to him—and possibly some sicko creeping around the house with her right now. But a greater part of her still didn't trust this strange redneck. For all she knew, he was the one that had left that message on her computer while she slept. Maybe he had even pushed the sheriff into the river.

"I'm fine," she said.

"You sure? Ain't that the sheriff's personal vehicle? What's he doin here?"

"None of your business. Go away."

He stood there a moment, looking honestly confused. "If you're okay, why don't you let me inside?"

"Please go away." Her voice cracked a little, and she hated herself for it.

Through the door's small window, Kelsea watched Russ scowl and stroke his mustache. She wasn't sure if he was angry or just thinking too hard.

"All right. Suit yerself. I was just tryna be a good neighbor." He spit a stream of brown liquid off to the side. "City pricks," he mumbled. He turned and ambled off to his Jeep.

After she watched the Jeep pull away, Kelsea sat down against the door to calm herself. At first she was relieved that he had left. But if he *wasn't* the person who had written that stuff on her computer, then she had turned away the only protection she might get.

The door shook against her back with a new knocking.

She forced herself to stand and look out the window. Relief surged through her when she saw James standing there. Kelsea unlocked and opened the door and fell onto his neck in a tight hug.

"Whoa. Everything all right?"

"James, something terrible is happening," she said into his shoulder.

"Are you okay? Do you need to go to the hospital?"

"No… I mean… I don't know if I'm okay, but I'm not hurt. Not yet. Come inside."

They sat on the couch. James studied Kelsea while she tried to figure out where to start.

"There was this girl," she said. "I don't know, she ran out into the woods, and I think she got lost. And then I drove to where I could call, and you didn't answer, and Russ helped me out of the snow, but then later he showed up and I thought it was him—and the sheriff—or he said he was; he wasn't in uniform, but he did have a badge—he fell in the river—"

"Whoa, slow down. What are you talking about? Who's in the river?"

Kelsea rubbed her eyes and took a breath. "Somehow the sheriff fell into the river and got trapped under the ice. He— he's dead. He was out looking for a girl I saw. Or… *thought* I saw. Now I'm not sure… but I'm really scared. And somebody was in the house while I was sleeping this afternoon."

"Show me."

"Huh?"

"Take me to the creek, where the person fell in. I need to see it, to be sure."

"But what if there's still someone in the house?"

"Why do you think someone else is in the house?"

"Hold on." Kelsea ran to the other room and brought her laptop back to show him the poem. "Here," she said, sitting next to him again and opening it up. "I was sleeping, and when I woke up I saw this—"

She stopped. Her document was still open, but the poem was gone.

"Saw what?"

"There… there was something else here, James. I'm serious. It was all creepy and weird. It said stuff about… bones or something."

"Settle down. You're sure you didn't just dream that?"

"I *know* it was there. It really freaked me out. It's why I ran out into the woods in the first place."

"But you also said you weren't sure about the girl."

"I know, but…" She sighed and shook her head. "Listen, maybe you think I'm some stupid ditz or something. And yeah, maybe I'm a little confused right now. But it was *there*."

James sighed. Kelsea could tell he didn't believe her. She felt her face turning red in frustration.

"Okay," he said, rubbing his forehead. "Well, just take me to the river."

She led him outside. The storm had settled down a lot, but the sky was still a solid gray blanket.

James looked up as they trudged along Kelsea's path through the yard. "It's resting now," he said. "But the people on The Weather Channel aren't too optimistic about the rest of the week."

TIMOTHY G. HUGUENIN

"You mean it could get worse?"

"Eh… who knows? You live in these mountains long enough, you learn not to trust the weather people. Things get all screwy here because of the topography. If my granny were still alive, I could give you a more definitive answer. Her knee always gave us a better forecast than those yahoos on TV. But it's also a pretty good rule of thumb to assume the worst, especially this time of year."

Kelsea looked straight ahead as they passed the shed and neared the trees. "And what would the worst be?" she said.

"Well, pretty bad. They're calling for a real whopper."

They got to the edge of the yard, and Kelsea leaned against a tree. "You mean this wasn't?"

James brushed snow off his jeans and smirked. "I mean, this wasn't anything to wink at. But nothing historic, either. Run-o'-the-mill winter around here. But they're calling for some big stuff in the next few days. A few years ago we had a storm so bad they shut a lot of the roads down." He said this almost in a bragging tone.

Probably exaggerating, Kelsea thought. She couldn't let herself think she would be stuck here any longer than she needed to be.

James pointed to Kelsea's footsteps through the woods. "This the way?"

"Yeah."

James took the lead, and she was fine with that. She really didn't want to be out here at all, much less see the drowned police officer. But she felt safer out here with James than she had alone in the house.

They came to the river, and James followed Kelsea's tracks to where the person had fallen through the ice. Kelsea stayed back a few feet.

James looked down into the river, and his face turned pale enough to match the snow. He staggered back and bent down with his hands on his knees. For a few seconds he looked like he was about to throw up, but he didn't.

"What do we do?" Kelsea asked.

James took a deep breath, then looked up, but not at Kelsea. His eyes went to the river and stayed there, his face twisted in a look of terror. "That's Coop, all right," he said. His voice sounded calm despite the expression on his face. "I don't think it's safe for us to try to get him out. Was there anyone else with him?"

"No, he's the only one who showed up. How could this have happened?"

James shook his head. His eyes were still locked on the creek, as if his gaze was trapped in the current with the dead sheriff. Kelsea didn't like it.

"Come on," he said, finally taking his eyes away from the top-frozen stream. "Let's get back to the house."

~

Kelsea sat on the couch in the living room while James started a fire. She was stunned and confused, and still a little leery of the house, although there hadn't been any more reason since the computer incident to think there was anyone else in here with them. She was doubting herself about that, now, too. She *had* just woken up when she thought she saw those words on the screen, after all.

You can't just dream or imagine something like that, she argued with herself. *Can you?*

At least James was here now. If anyone *was* lurking in the house's dark corners, she felt safer now that she had a friend.

"What do we do?" she asked.

"Well, I was thinking," James said as he worked on the fire. "I brought a lasagna and a bottle of wine. They're still in the truck—"

"What? How can you be thinking of dinner?"

He looked at her for a second and then looked away. "Kelsea, I really don't think any lurkers are in the house."

"But there *was* a little girl out there in the cold. And… in the river, the…" She faltered, not wanting to feel the words *dead body* on her tongue. "Shouldn't we do something?"

He blew on the fire and stood. "That should do it," he said, ignoring her question. "Still may be a tad chilly for a few minutes, but it'll warm right up. I'll make some cocoa." He walked to the kitchen.

What is with this guy? Kelsea thought. *Is this how everyone around here acts after finding a dead person?*

She heard James put the kettle on the stove, then returned and leaned against the wall. He ran a hand through his hair. "Okay, listen. If there *was* a girl, like you said, and if she *has* been out there for this long… well, I'm sorry to say this, but she's gone. And the sheriff… I don't know, Kelsea. It's not like we can help him now, either."

"We have to call someone."

"Do you have cell service here?"

She checked her phone, even though she already knew the answer. "No, I guess... But can't we like, drive to the station or something?"

He shook his head. "Sorry, out of the question. The sheriff's office is down in Parsons. Roads are way too bad right now to get down the mountain. I almost didn't make it here from my house, and that's a pretty short drive. But I'll tell you what. I'll drive back over to the house and make a call on the landline while the lasagna cooks. But other than that... I don't really know what else we can do." James rubbed his forehead. He looked more scared than he was trying to sound, the same way he had been acting back at the river.

Kelsea wondered if there was something he wasn't telling her. She remembered the way he had looked at that river, as if it were a living beast that was sleeping, and the slightest sound or movement could wake it and invite its fury upon them.

She looked down at her hands and noticed she had been clenching them tightly together, as if in prayer. She loosened them and watched the blood rush back into her fingers.

James went out to the truck and came back with the lasagna and wine. He avoided eye contact with Kelsea as he walked past to put the lasagna in the oven.

"James. Tell me what's going on."

He walked to the front door. "I'm going to my house so I can use the phone. I'll be back in a bit."

"Hold on. You're not leaving me here alone, not after all this." Her breathing quickened slightly. She took some deep breaths.

"Don't worry, Kelsea. I don't think you're in any danger. Just stay inside."

She wanted to argue, but she didn't want to look weak, either. "Fine." But she didn't feel fine.

At last he met her eyes. "I'll handle everything."

She felt she didn't have a choice but to trust him.

"See you soon," he said, and he left.

She watched out the window as he drove off. The light was already getting low outside. She felt an ache in her chest.

It gets dark so fast in these damn hills. God, I miss LA.

A shriek from the kitchen made her jump—but it was just the tea kettle. She turned it off and poured the water into a mug that James had already filled with hot cocoa mix. She sat down and sipped on it.

James was right. There was no bringing back the sheriff. And the girl—well, Kelsea could only hope that she had found her way safely back to her own house; she couldn't bear to consider the alternative. Either way, it was too late now.

She needed something to keep her mind off of all that had happened today. She picked up her laptop and opened her article. Marge was probably losing her hair waiting for this thing. Kelsea knew she would need to finish it tonight and take it to TipTop tomorrow morning so she could email it, and she wasn't looking forward to the deluge of angry voicemails, texts, and emails that would undoubtedly be waiting for her when she was able to connect to the outside world again.

There was a mental state that Kelsea would sometimes

enter when writing, a kind of self-hypnosis in which time was lost and words poured steadily from her like water from a faucet. She privately called this "hitting the groove." The groove did not come easy at first, not with the girl and the drowned sheriff weighing on her mind. But she could do nothing now but wait for James to call the station and return. She concentrated hard on the article, and after a while the faucet of words began to drip, and then it trickled, and then it flowed.

Kelsea was giving her finished article a second read-over when she smelled something burning. She looked up to see smoke seeping out of the oven.

"No!" She jumped up, shut the oven off, and pulled the lasagna out. It looked like a black lump of coal. She put the ruined dish on the counter and fanned the clouds of smoke away from her face.

Where is James? I'm going to kill him when he gets back.

She checked her computer for the time and saw that he had been gone for over an hour. It was already dark outside, the sky as black as their burnt dinner.

She was hungry now, despite her fear, but she couldn't eat this garbage. She didn't feel like cooking, but she wasn't going to keep waiting around for James to return before she ate. She remembered her leftover burrito, and she ate it with a glass of the wine James had left behind. It was a strange pairing, but somehow it seemed to fit.

She made the last corrections on her article and shut her

computer down for the night. Freed from the comforting bondage of her computer screen, her nerves were returning in full force.

James had said the roads were bad. What if he had wrecked on the way to his house? With no cell phone access out here, there was no way for her to know.

She tried not to worry—an impossible task given the day's events—but she couldn't sit around twiddling her thumbs while he was out. With her magazine article finished, she needed a new distraction. And even though it was dark out, it wasn't nearly late enough to go to sleep. She went to the study, flipped on the light, and started sorting through all the clutter on the writing desk.

Barely legible notes on paper scraps were strewn about the desk in an eerie resemblance to Kelsea's own work area. A few thin paperbacks were stacked on one corner of the desk. On another corner a handful of ballpoint pens were stashed in a blue coffee mug with *WEST VIRGINIA UNIVERSITY* printed on it in gold letters. A blue tin beside the mug read *Edgeworth Ready-Rubbed*; she opened it to find an old stash of pipe tobacco, smelling earthy and sweet. Since she didn't smoke, she shut the tin and tossed it into one of the black trash bags.

A spiral-bound notebook was buried under all the scrap paper in the middle of the desk. On the cover was written *MILES HENDRICKS* in that shaky block script of old men. This was the name of the man who had been responsible for her birth—and her life without a family.

Kelsea opened the notebook. Dates and notes peppered

the pages between lines of free verse. Apparently Miles had been a poet, or fancied himself one. Kelsea glanced back at the paperbacks and noticed one of them bore his name on its spine. She pulled it out from between collections by T. S. Eliot and Wendell Berry.

Allegheny Mist: A Collection of Poems by Miles Hendricks.

She opened it to a page that had its corner folded over. The poem on the page was titled "Little One." It was short, only six lines, and it spoke of a young daughter whom the poet had loved and lost early.

Kelsea threw the book across the room. "If you loved me so much you could have kept me," she said aloud. She stuffed the notebook in the trash with the rest of the junk on the desk.

There were more spiral-bound notebooks stuffed in the desk drawer, along with miscellaneous bills and receipts, pens and paperclips, indicator species typical of the old desk ecosystem. She trashed these as well.

She thought she had all of the desk cleaned out, but when she slid all the drawers out one last time just to be sure, she saw something in the track behind the bottom drawer. She reached in and pulled it out.

It was a photograph of herself as a young girl. She was standing on the deck outside this house, wearing a yellow summer dress and a smile as full of life as the green trees behind her.

Both sides of the picture were torn off. The girl's arms reached both ways, cut short at the wrists by the ragged edges.

This was the companion to the picture on the mantel in the living room.

Kelsea thought about throwing it away, but she couldn't. Instead, she walked over to the book she had thrown, smoothed out the pages that had folded over when it landed. She flipped to "Little One" and placed the photograph there. She closed the book and set it back on the desk.

She looked once more around the room. She would need to clean out all the remaining books on the shelves, too—donate them to the library or something.

The telephone on the wall rang. Kelsea stared at it, confused. She didn't think it was still connected—wasn't that why James had left, to use the working landline at his house?

Warily, she picked up the phone and held it to her ear. "Hello?"

The phone answered with static. She was about to hang up when she heard a man's voice coming through. It was soft, nearly drowned out by the static, but he said her name, unmistakably.

"James, is that you? I can't… you're not coming through very well."

More static. Then, "Kelsea…" again.

Then the line went dead.

Kelsea hung up the phone.

She told herself it had been James; he had called to let her know why he never came back. It had been James, it *only* could have been James, and that was that.

She went back to cleaning, because she knew if she

thought about the call too much she would have to come to terms with the fact that the voice, although certainly male, certainly had not been James's.

~

She dusted and swept the rest of the study, collected all the books into trash bags, and explored the rest of the ground floor. There were a few other guest bedrooms, and with the discovery of each, Kelsea felt a greater twinge of resentment. *All these rooms, and still no room for their "Little One."* But she moved through them quickly, as there was little in them but the furniture, and not much to clean.

In the center of the house were the master bedroom and its connected bathroom. For a reason she couldn't understand, the sight of the bathroom door gave her chills.

She would start with the bedroom first. The two bureaus were full of stale-smelling, moth-eaten clothes, which she stuffed into trash bags. A walk-in closet held some old dresses, men's shirts, and sport coats. These, too, she discarded, except for one charcoal-colored wool peacoat that fit her almost perfectly. It smelled a little funky, but it was in good condition and would be a lot warmer than the thin jacket she had now. She threw it on the bed while she cleaned the rest of the room.

She cleaned furiously and without much thought, because she couldn't afford to think about the body under the ice, or about James's unfulfilled promise to return for dinner, or about that bathroom—what *was* it about that bathroom?

All the knick-knacks went swiftly into black trash bags. The only items she didn't throw out were the pieces of jewelry on top of one of the bureaus. None of the jewelry was her style, but for some reason she couldn't trash it.

I'll sell them or something, she told herself. *They're probably worth something.*

She finally forced herself to go into the bathroom. She saw nothing about the room itself that made sense of that ominous feeling. But when her eyes came to rest on the tub, a small pit formed in her stomach, an inexplicable feeling of fear and nausea combined with a strong sensation of déjà vu.

As she cleaned, she tried to shrug off that horrible feeling, but it was like a monster clawing at the locked door of some dark room in her mind. The door in her head looked a lot like that bathroom door, too, except it was red as blood. She was very relieved when she finished with the bathroom and was able to move on.

It was late into the night when she finished dusting, sweeping, and mopping the entirety of the downstairs. It was now sparkling and spotless, apart from the trash bags lining the halls, and she was exhausted. The cleaning had at least passed the time and caused her to temporarily forget the nightmares of the day. And while she was still worried about James's absence,

but he called, that was him *calling, to say something happened but he's all right*

her body, having used up its adrenaline, was finally crashing.

She thought about sleeping in the same room where she

had napped before, but she wanted to be close to the door in case James returned. So she went back to the living room and put some more logs on the fire before falling asleep on the couch for the second night in a row.

Chapter Nine

Kelsea was in her old bedroom, looking at the dollhouse. She was having trouble controlling her thoughts and had even less control over her body.

I must be dreaming.

She gave in and let her subconscious lead her.

Her legs stepped slowly toward the dollhouse. Her hand reached out, and her fingers traced the incredibly detailed wood-carved shingles. She remembered now that the dollhouse had been a Christmas gift from her parents, her most loved possession. She thought of those wooden chains hanging in the shed. She wondered if Miles had made the dollhouse himself.

A small hand tugged on her shirt. Her body turned her around, and standing before her was a young girl: the girl in the ripped photograph.

Me.

Her barely lucid mind recognized that the girl's dress was yellow, like the one worn by the girl she had seen in the woods. But why should this surprise her? This was standard fare for dreams.

There was something else familiar about the dress—but this thought slipped from her clouded mind's grasp when the younger Kelsea grabbed her hand and pulled her out of the room and down the stairs.

"Wait," she said to her dream-girl-self, but the words came out slowly and echoed strangely in her ears.

They went out the back door and into the yard. The wind whipped Kelsea's hair in her face, and without a coat or shoes on, every muscle in her body tensed in the frigid dark night. Ahead, soft yellow light fell through cracks in the shed and crawled across the yard in thin shafts.

Young Kelsea pulled her toward it.

Her bare feet ached in the snow. She meant to speak, but all that came out was a low whine.

The light from the shed's single bulb hurt her eyes. She put a hand up as she entered. The plywood floor was rough and splintery, and dust and cobwebs stuck to her wet toes. At least she was no longer walking through snow.

Young Kelsea reached under the shelves and pulled out the green wooden box. She lifted one end and looked at the older Kelsea without speaking.

Regardless of Kelsea's will, her body squatted down and lifted the other end of the box. It was lighter than she had expected.

They carried the box back into the house. Clumps of wet snow fell from Kelsea's pants onto the floor as they went up the stairs. The girl led them to her bedroom, and together they put the box under one of the tiny beds.

Why are there two beds? Kelsea tried to ask the girl, but only empty breath came from her lungs.

~

Kelsea sat straight up on the couch, cold and sweaty and panting.

What a weird dream.

She looked around. There was no girl. The embers in the fireplace glowed faintly.

She lay back down and wrapped herself tightly in the blanket, too lazy

and a bit too spooked, let's be honest

to get up and add wood to the fire. She could hear the gas heat come on, so she knew it was still working, but somehow she was cold to her bones. She fell asleep again, and this time she didn't dream.

Chapter Ten

Kelsea woke late in the morning. She rose from the couch, groggy and cold and unwilling, and trudged to the upstairs bathroom for a shower—very long and *very* hot.

Refreshed from her shower, she now noticed something she had missed when she had gotten up: small drips of water trailing down the hall. She followed the drips to her childhood bedroom, where they ended in a small puddle. Then she followed the drips the other way, and they led down the stairs, then stretched in both directions. The drips were larger in the direction of the clock room, forming tiny puddles.

They're tracks of melted snow. Someone came in through the back doors.

She walked to the living room. A wave of nausea washed over her when she saw that the tracks stopped at the couch. She couldn't help but picture old Russ Pifer standing over her as she slept, brown drool leaking from the corner of his puffed-out lower lip, then creeping back the way he had come.

He could still be in the house.

Kelsea grabbed the fireplace poker and crept back down the hall, following the drips of water past the stairs. The trail went straight to the French doors. And she didn't see anyone hiding under the pool table or anything.

She looked through the glass doors at the shed in the blowing snow.

The light was on.

Kelsea's dream came back to her, and for a second she wondered…

No. It couldn't have been *real.*

But clearly someone had come in and out of here, and there was no mistaking the light coming from the shed right now. Kelsea supposed it *could* have been her. She didn't have a history of sleepwalking, but there was a first for everything. Or maybe she just *wanted* to believe that explanation. It was better than thinking Russ or some other whacko had broken in while she slept.

She put on the old wool peacoat and shoes, went out to the shed, and shut off the light. She stood there for a moment in the darkness, listening to the wind whistle through the cracks in the walls.

She thought she heard something move in the back corner. But it was probably her imagination. Or the wind blowing a piece of paper. Or a mouse. Or something. Whatever it was didn't require her turning the light back on to find out. Whatever it was probably would be better left alone, and she had better get back to the house.

Inside, she locked the back doors. All of a sudden she didn't want to stay; she didn't feel safe here. She remembered what James had said last night about the roads. If they were really that bad, maybe she shouldn't be out.

But I have *to get out. I have to do* something *to get a grip.*

Her eyes fell on one of the trash bags. *That's it. I'll find a place in town to dump this stuff. And coffee. Coffee always helps.*

She made a few hurried trips in and out to take all the bags of trash and books into the truck. She was making one last look around to make sure she had gotten everything when she noticed Miles's book of poetry on the desk. On an impulse she didn't quite understand, she put the book in her purse. Then she left the house, making sure she had the key before locking the front door.

The presence of the sheriff's Subaru in her driveway sent another jolt of panic through her system, and she forced it down. James had said he would take care of things. The police would be here any minute, and the woods behind the house would be marked a crime scene. She would probably spend most of the day giving her statement, answering questions—not that she knew much about what had happened. The whole thing was a nightmare.

They'll want me to lead them to the body.

She couldn't go back to the river, couldn't have that image rebranded onto her mind. She knew she shouldn't leave, but right now, she *had* to get away from this house. Go to town, do some ordinary errands, and try to pretend, at least for a few hours, that her life was normal.

The road really was terrible. She crawled her way to town, never taking the truck out of four-wheel drive.

Though her knuckles were white and her blood was pumping from the terror of navigating the slippery, winding road, she felt some comfort in thinking that the conditions might explain James's absence last night, and why no more cops had shown up yet.

Her phone occasionally buzzed in her purse as it hit pockets of service on the way to town and voicemails and texts came through. In stop-and-go LA traffic, she would have been tempted to check them; on this slippery mountain road, that temptation was easy to resist. She kept her eyes straight ahead.

At TipTop, she ordered a macchiato and sat down at a table with her laptop.

As soon as she connected to the wifi, her inbox blew up. Most of the emails were from Marge, with subject headings full of question marks, exclamation points, and a few swear words. She deleted all of these without reading them. Then she attached the article to a new message and sent it with just a few lines:

Sorry for the delay. I told you, hard to connect with the outside world here. Long day yesterday. You don't even know. But it's done. — K. S.

She sighed. *I don't like this any more than you do, Marge. Just give me a break here while I resist a nervous breakdown.*

A girl just a few years younger than Kelsea set the macchiato down on the table.

"Thanks," Kelsea said.

"No problem."

The girl walked back behind the counter. Kelsea watched

her, wondering if she lived here on her own, and how she made her rent on a barista's paycheck, and why on God's green earth any person would put herself through such torment.

She had to admit, though, this little town did have a certain kind of charm. But still, without a decent salary, or some means to travel often and escape cabin fever, she couldn't imagine actually living here. She had only been here a few days, and it was already too much.

Then again, she had been through some pretty crazy stuff.

She sipped her beverage and tried to get her bearings. What had happened yesterday? To the girl in the woods? To the sheriff? To James?

She checked her voicemails, deleting one after another from her editor. She almost deleted the last one, then realized that it wasn't from Marge, but from James, sent last night. She put the phone close to her ear and let it play.

"Hey, Kelsea. Sorry about everything. I'm at my house, but I won't be able to get back to you tonight. I guess you won't get this for a while… which is terrible, because you're either going to be really mad at me or really worried, or maybe both, I don't know. Anyways. Some trouble with my truck—I was going a little too fast, slid into a tree. Truck's pretty messed up. I'm fine though. Walked the rest of the way to my house. Hopefully you can somehow get this tonight and pick me up, but I doubt it. Tomorrow I'll call Craig up for a tow, but until then I guess I'm stuck here. See you when I see you."

So that was *him calling last night. He must have tried the house after he left this voicemail.*

A wave of relief washed over her. An unfortunate accident, but he was okay. It explained everything except why more police hadn't shown up—surely he would have called them. But at least he was still around to help her figure out what to do.

She almost called him back immediately, then decided against it. Let *him* worry this time, a little payback for leaving her in that house alone. She would drive to his house after her errands to ask him about the police. She reminded herself that James knew the way people around here did things; he would know the best way to sort all this out. *I'll handle everything,* he had said.

She blew a nervous lungful of air between pursed lips. *He's probably at the house even now, showing the police the sheriff's body.*

She felt sick thinking of the sheriff, twisted strangely and pressed against a rock under the ice. She forced the image from her head.

James will take care of it.

In the meantime, she would focus on her errands.

She Googled realty companies in the area and called a few of them. The first two didn't answer their phones, but the third one did.

"Hi, my name is Kelsea Stone, I have a house in Canaan Valley that I'm thinking about selling. Or maybe a vacation rental or something."

"Great!" said a female voice on the other end of the line.

The woman's perkiness was slightly annoying but lifted Kelsea's spirits at the same time. "Let's set up a meeting. Can you come by our office sometime today? Eleven thirty?"

Kelsea bit her lip. She would have to find a way to kill an hour and a half in town, but it would be better than making an extra trip. "Sure."

"Great, I'll see you then. Kelsea... what was it again?"

"Stone. Like a rock."

"Okeydokey!" the woman said. "Looking forward to it! Bye!"

"Thanks, bye."

Kelsea sat and looked out the window while she drank her espresso. A few cars drove down the one-way road, some with skis and snowboards racked on top.

She finished her drink with plenty of time before her meeting. She thought about walking around town to kill time, but it was warm inside, and she wasn't ready to go back into the cold. She glanced down and noticed Miles's book poking out of her purse. She pulled it out and studied the cover. It featured a picture of a forested canyon blazing in autumn colors; she was sure it had to be digitally enhanced. She opened to the first poem—"Cheat River Song in My Pocket"—and read.

~

"You okay, ma'am?"

"Huh?" Kelsea looked up from the book. The barista had taken her mug and was looking at her with concern.

"You, uh... you were crying. I just was wondering if everything was okay."

"Oh." Kelsea wiped her cheek, and her hand came back wet. She felt her cheeks burn in embarrassment. "I'm fine. Thanks. It's nothing."

"Okay. Well, let me know if you need anything."

"Sure. Thanks."

As Kelsea stuffed the book back into her purse, the picture she had stuck in it fell out. She reached under the table and picked it up. She hadn't noticed before, but a name and year were written in pencil on the back. The year was from just before they sent her away. But the name was wrong.

Kayla.

Kelsea scrunched her face in confusion. The writing was in the same shaky block letters she had seen in Miles's notebook. *He forgot my* name? Her feelings morphed from confusion to hurt and anger.

They had discarded her, their only daughter, like a bag of rotten onions. Why bother to remember her name, right? She had ditched theirs, after all. No big deal. The feeling was mutual.

She shoved the picture into her purse and stormed outside to the truck. She couldn't understand why this was all coming out now. She had always been such a stoic, had never thought this stuff even *mattered* much to her. Strength, independence—these were her core, her life. She didn't know anything else. Didn't *remember* anything else— honestly, even her days bouncing around foster homes were a bit of a blur. She didn't—*shouldn't*—care who her parents were or what they had thought about her.

But as she stood there leaning against the truck, clenching her teeth and her hands and eyes, she realized that maybe all this stuff had just been bottled up inside her, buried so deep that she hadn't even known it was there, until now. Discovering these remnants of her family was unearthing a whole new part of her that she had long ignored.

She checked the time. It was still too early to meet the realtor.

Too embarrassed to go back inside, she went in search of a library.

The library was little more than a vinyl-sided singlewide stuffed with a motley arrangement of books and a few old computers huddled in a corner.

An impossibly tall white-haired woman greeted Kelsea with a smile. "Howdy. Ain't from around here?"

"Um, no. But I just inherited a place nearby, and it had all these books, so… Do you mind if I leave them with you?"

"Naw, sure. We love donations. Bring 'em on in."

Kelsea had three bags full of books in the truck, and she brought them in one at a time.

"Well by golly," the librarian said. Her eyes were wide, apparently surprised at all the books this strange woman was discarding, and perhaps a bit appalled that she had chosen to transport them loosely in large black trash bags. Until that moment, Kelsea hadn't considered the judgment a librarian might cast on her for not taking better care.

"Well, so…" she said. "There they are."

"Why, thank ya," the woman said, opening one of the bags and looking into it. "Mighty wide of ya."

"Sure, no problem." Kelsea felt incredibly uncomfortable and awkward and wasn't completely sure why. "Listen, is there a place around here I can take my trash?"

The lady looked up to the corner and cocked her head. "Town dump. But you gotta pay. Except for the free day every month. But that's done passed." She paused. "I reckon I could take what you got now and the garbage man will get it next week. Ain't sayin I'll take all your trash *later*. Just sayin, what you got *now*—leave it set outside, next to the steps."

Kelsea nodded. "Thanks a lot."

"Don't mention it. Thanks for the books."

Kelsea went out to her truck and moved her trash bags from its bed to a spot next to the library's front steps. The librarian stepped outside and leaned her bony lower hip on the railing, lit a cigarette and took a drag from it and then said, "Say, where's your place?"

"Oh, out in Canaan Valley."

"Ah." The woman frowned knowingly and nodded. "Nice place, huh?"

"Sure. A bit of work needed. But I'm hoping to make it into a vacation rental."

"Yeah, them rich folk outta DC and whatnot like to come here. You said you inherited the place? Who was yer folks? I mighta known 'em."

Kelsea felt uncomfortable with the woman's prying, but she answered anyway. "Miles and Darlene Hendricks."

The lady didn't say anything, just returned a blank look. She had lifted her cigarette halfway to her face and now just held it there, her body frozen, a thin strand of smoke twirling up from the end of the cigarette. Kelsea wondered if she had offended the woman somehow. She remembered the sign in the driveway that some kid had amended to say *CRAZY Hendricks's Place*. Maybe that reputation was better known among the people here than she had thought; maybe this woman assumed that whatever madness supposedly afflicted Miles and Darlene had been passed down to their daughter.

"I, uh, I never knew my parents though. Didn't even know they had died until the lawyer called me."

The lady blinked, still silent. She dropped the cigarette on the step and extinguished it under her canvas tennis shoe.

Well, at least she's done nosing into my business, Kelsea thought. "Well, I'll see you later." She waved awkwardly.

The lady nodded and kept staring. Kelsea shrugged off the woman's cold eyes and got into the truck. The librarian turned and ducked back inside when Kelsea drove out of the lot.

A tiny bell rang above the door as Kelsea stepped into the real estate office. A heavyset, middle-aged woman walked over from a coffeemaker with a mug in her hand. "Kelsea Stone, right? I'm Sarah; I believe we spoke on the phone."

She smiled warmly and stuck out a hand. Kelsea shook it. The woman's skin was soft and plump.

"Yes. Nice to meet you."

"Let's sit and talk."

Sarah led Kelsea to her desk, and they both took a seat. "Alrighty. So you said you have a house in Canaan you want to rent out. Tell me about the place. What's the address? I'll see if I can pull it up on the computer."

The address. Kelsea did a mental facepalm and answered, "I wrote it down, but I left it in the truck. I can't remember. Honestly, my biological parents passed it down to me, but I never really knew them, and I only just found out. It's off some driveway on that main stretch there. Um…"

"Who were your folks? I don't recall anyone with the name of Stone living in the area."

"No. I changed my last name. The house was owned by Miles and Darlene Hendricks."

Sarah's smile fell away to an expression identical to the one worn by that old librarian just minutes ago.

Kelsea shifted in her seat. "Is, uh, is something wrong?"

Sarah stood slowly from her chair. "I'm afraid I won't be able to help you," she said stiffly. "Please leave."

"Are you serious?" Kelsea said.

"We can't help you here," Sarah repeated solemnly. "You can try someone else, if you want. But we aren't interested in representing that property."

Kelsea stood. She wanted to say something smart, felt her middle finger wanting to rise in salute to the woman's fantastic service, but she held her temper down and painted on a candy-sweet smile. "Well, thanks so much anyway," she said. She did an about face and walked quickly out of the building.

What now? There was clearly something about her family that was odious to these people. She thought about trying again to contact the other realtors. But after being rebuffed mysteriously by the old librarian and now Sarah, Kelsea assumed she would face similar responses from everyone else.

She hopped into the truck, shifted into reverse, and punched the gas a little too hard. The tires spun, and she zipped out of her parking spot right in the path of an oncoming car. The driver of the car laid on his horn and his brakes, sliding to a stop only inches from Kelsea.

The red-faced driver screamed at her. Kelsea didn't care. She put the truck in drive and headed out of town. She needed to know what all this was about. And there was only one person she could go to for answers.

Chapter Eleven

Kelsea knocked on James's door a little harder than she meant to. She heard a muffled "Coming," and a few seconds later the door opened.

"Kelsea! So you got my message. Listen—"

"No, *you* listen," she said, cutting him off. James raised his eyebrows as she continued. "What the hell is going on that you're not telling me? Why didn't more police come last night? Why is everyone in town acting so *weird*?"

James looked around nervously. "Come inside," he whispered.

She stepped in, and James closed the door softly behind her. The house's warmth took some of the edge off of her mood, even though she didn't want it to. There was a comforting goldenness to the house's atmosphere. A mug of coffee, a sandwich, and an issue of the *Wall Street Journal* sat on an oak dining table. James pulled a chair out for her and they sat down. In the corner of the room was the grandfather clock.

"You haven't gotten the clock fixed?"

"Huh?"

She pointed to it. "You said you were going to send it to a guy to get it fixed."

"Oh. Yeah. I've had a bunch of stuff going on with my clients. Haven't been able to get in touch with him yet."

"Okay," she said, trying to recover all the pissed-off-ness she'd had before sitting down. "So tell me what's going on here. Did you call the police last night?"

"Yes—"

"Then why didn't they show? James, a man *died* out there yesterday!"

"Calm down," James said, "I heard there was some big rockfall last night on the road outside of Parsons, between the station and here. It's cutting off all traffic up and down the mountain. I'm sure the police will be here once it's cleared."

"You think they'll get it cleared today?"

"I don't know. But I called someone else, too." He met her eyes for a second before looking away, toward the grandfather clock. "I think you might be right about not being alone at the house," he added slowly.

Kelsea felt sick at the idea of someone watching her there. "No... I was imagining that. You said it yourself. I must have typed that stuff up in my sleep. It was just nerves."

"I don't think there's a prowler, or anything like that," James said. "I don't think... I don't think it's a *who* as much as it's a... um... a *what*, maybe. I don't even know if you could call it a *what*."

"That's what I thought too, for a while. But I haven't

found any scat or hair or anything like that in the house. So I can't figure—"

"No, I'm not talking about an animal."

Kelsea narrowed her eyes. "Then what *are* you talking about?"

James finally looked her in the eye. "I think there's a spirit in your house. Something malevolent. A demon."

Kelsea crossed her arms and blew a sigh through pursed lips. "Oh, boy."

"Listen, I know it sounds like a bunch of hocus-pocus," James said. "I didn't want to believe it myself. I saw signs of it, before you got here, but I just ignored them and convinced myself it was my imagination. Even after you told me about the stuff with your computer, I didn't want to believe it. But when we saw Coop out there—"

"A man fell in the river, and you're blaming *ghosts*? James, it was an accident. He tripped or something, and got… got stuck."

James nodded. "Maybe. But what if it wasn't? If there *is* a demon… Do you want to take that risk?"

"I don't believe this." Kelsea laughed, but it came out sounding more nervous than she intended it. As she thought back on all the strange occurrences, it was tempting to see it James's way.

"I understand," James said. "I'm like you: I always look for the most rational explanation. But with all I've seen… and I hope I'm wrong, really… but right now I can't escape the feeling—the *conviction*, I guess you might say—that the old Hendricks place is possessed."

There was a moment of silence between them. Then Kelsea put her hand on the table and stood. "No," she said.

"Kelsea—"

"No. I don't know what your game is here. But frankly, I've had enough of it. I still have too much to do this week before my flight. And God knows if I'll be able to get this place off my hands, the way that realtor was treating me. This is unreal." She walked to the door.

"I called a priest," James said.

She turned. He looked sincerely worried.

"Just let us come over this evening. I still have to make up that lasagna to you. Then the priest can take a look around the house, sprinkle water and burn some sage, or whatever priests do. If there's nothing there, there's nothing there." He sighed. "At any rate, I don't suggest you staying the night there until it's all figured out."

He had a point there. Demons or not, the place did spook her out, especially with the sheriff still in the woods. Maybe booking a hotel wasn't a bad idea.

"I'll call Black Bear tonight," she said, fully understanding that he had expected her to stay at his place.

"Okay." The disappointment was clear on his face. "That's good, then. You want to use my land line before you leave?"

"Oh, I'll use the phone at my place."

"Won't work, remember? The service has been shut off for months."

"That wasn't you trying to call me last night?"

James's face was solemn. "There's no way you could have gotten a call on that phone. And I *know* I didn't call that number."

Kelsea felt her neck tingle. "Seriously, James. The phone rang last night. I picked it up. Someone said my name. It was staticky and hard to hear, but it was definitely a man saying my name. And I know I didn't imagine it."

James shook his head slowly. "Father Marco," he said. "That's his name—the priest I called. We'll be over around five. Don't worry about picking me up; Father Marco will give me a ride. I'll bring dinner again."

Kelsea shrugged, trying to appear nonchalant. She couldn't accept this; he must be mistaken about the phone and the rest of this. They needed cops, not ghostbusters.

She opened the front door. The cloud cover had darkened. A sharp wind pierced her.

"One more thing," James said. "I've been looking for a key I lost. It must have fallen out of my pocket when we were carrying the clock. It's kind of an old style. Looks like a crown on one end."

He was talking about the key she had found taped to the inside of the clock. It was probably still in her other pants; she had completely forgotten about it. But why would he have said it fell from his own pocket?

"I haven't seen any key," she said.

"Okay. Well, be on the lookout. It goes to something private to me. Valuable."

"Sure," Kelsea said.

She shut the door without saying goodbye and drove back to the house.

~

Kelsea went about cleaning the upper floor of the house. Once in a while, when she took a break, that eerie being-watched feeling returned to her, but she now found it easier to push aside. She was getting used to it, and all the talk of demon activity actually made her less prone to scaring. Somehow hearing James say that kind of thing out loud made her own paranoia more obviously ridiculous. Spooky feelings were no more than an over-suggestible imagination. Chemicals and irrationality. That was all. This dusty hardwood floor was solid, real. Sweeping and mopping it grounded her to reality. She stood on *fact*. Possibly valuable fact, if she could find a good realty company. She knew she wouldn't have time to manage the property herself from LA, but surely there was somebody around here that would do it. The lady she had met—what was her name? Sarah—what a kook! They couldn't *all* be like that; surely there were some professionals in this town, *somewhere*. She had thought James to be an exception, a diamond in a heap of coal, but she was beginning to rethink that.

She rested on her mop handle, stretched the tightness from her back, and smiled.

Evil spirits. *Right.*

As if in response to her thoughts, she felt the temperature drop suddenly.

My imagination. I worked up some sweat doing this floor and got a chill when I stopped to rest. No spirits, just thermodynamics.

She bent over and continued to clean.

It was getting close to five o'clock, and the light coming in through the windows was dimming fast. Kelsea flipped light switches on as she went. She was making good progress, and felt she would probably be done soon. She hoped that James and his priest friend would be late, or that their visit would be quick (or both), so that she could finish up and be done with this house tonight. The police still hadn't come by— that rockfall must really have been severe.

She found some more pictures of Miles and Darlene. In one of them, they sat somber-faced on the couch in the living room, gray showing on their temples, a banner behind them reading *Happy Anniversary*, a few friends in the background, and half of James's face cut off in the corner of the photo. In another they stood as a young couple on a deck in front of a full waterfall—it was Blackwater Falls; Kelsea remembered seeing a postcard of the place in the gas station. In another, Miles sat outside the house in a rocking chair, smoking a pipe, smiling at something off camera. Kelsea wondered if he was smiling at her, if they had again ripped her out of the photo before framing it, just as they had ripped her out of their lives.

She threw the photos in the trash, frames and all.

One of the rooms upstairs shocked her with a scary menagerie of shadow monsters until she turned on the lights. Animals were stuffed and mounted in various configurations— all dead, all harmless. Guns of various hunting calibers were hung all over the wall between the animals.

She wasn't sure yet what she would do with the animals and the guns. Some people might get a kick out of it. But she wouldn't be able to rent the place out to any vegans. For now, she would just dust everything and leave it the way it was until she had a better idea.

Between two windows was a photo of a hunter dressed in camo and blaze orange, holding up the amply antlered head of a buck. She stepped closer and was surprised to see that Darlene was the hunter in the photo, not Miles. There were soft lines around her eyes, and although her blond hair was losing its radiance, it had not yet gone full white. Her smile was full of pride. Yet there was still sadness in her eyes.

The only pictures in which the two looked purely happy were those taken when they were young. It was as if after Kelsea left, they lost some sort of spark.

Another room, this one full of quilts. They were everywhere, hanging on the walls, hanging from the ceiling, draped over racks and chairs. They had collected a lot of dust, and as Kelsea pushed her way through the quilts she stirred it up and sneezed violently.

She discovered a sewing machine tucked in one corner of the room hidden by baskets stacked high and overflowing with cloth and tools.

Kelsea groaned. *And what am I going to do with all this?*

An image came to her, much like the ones of Miles in the study and herself with the dollhouse, but this time of Darlene: hunched over the sewing machine, hair pulled back and wrapped up in a head scarf, pins sticking out from her lips, cloth flowing out from the churning sewing machine and cascading to the floor like a waterfall. Behind Darlene hung two identical little dresses, similar to the one that

Kelsea had been wearing in the old photo.

Two dresses. Two beds.

Kelsea felt something brush against her rear. She jumped and spun. A quilt hanging from the ceiling waved slightly as if someone had just run up against it from the other side. She felt her heart leap into her throat.

Steeling herself, she pulled the quilt back like a curtain— but there was no one, just a window that was opened a few inches. A soft but icy breeze blew on her face.

No wonder it's so cold in here.

She walked over to the window and pushed down on it. It was old and swollen and was stuck hard, and she leaned down with all her weight until it finally gave and slammed shut with a loud, hammer-like sound. The cracked glass rattled in its frame.

She sneezed again, then weaved her way through the maze of cloth and back into the hallway, shutting the door behind her. That room was a whole project in itself. She would have to come back to it tomorrow, when she had more time.

That left only one other room uncleaned: her old bedroom. She wondered if her subconscious had deliberately guided her to come to it last, as if there was something in that room that would uncover memories she didn't want to confront.

She was just heading for the bedroom door when there was a knock downstairs. She was surprised to find herself relieved to have to put off cleaning that final room.

James and another man stood at the door. James held a dish, from which rose the smell of warm pasta and cheese.

Behind them all was dark but for the thick snowflakes that fell into the light shining through the open doorway.

"Kelsea," James said, "meet Father Marco Giannantonio. Father, Kelsea Stone. Formerly Hendricks."

The priest was short and round, with an honest smile. Kelsea had expected him to come dressed in something clerical—a collar or robe or something—but he stood before her in a brown faux leather coat over a baby blue polo and jeans, his head covered by a nondescript winter knit cap. His trimmed salt-and-pepper goatee wore traces of the snow that was now falling heavily behind the two men. A black leather bag hung from the crook of his arm like a purse.

"Nice to meet you, Father Giannantonio," Kelsea said.

He shook her hand in both of his, and the bag swung back and forth. "Please, call me Father Marco," he said, with no trace of the Italian that Kelsea had assumed would be thick in his speech. Instead he spoke with a West Virginia accent, less subtle than James's, but not overbearing. "'Father Giannantonio' is too stuffy, too hard to say."

"Okay, Father Marco it is," Kelsea said. "Come inside."

"I cooked the lasagna in advance this time," James said as he set the dish on the table and pulled back the foil. Curls of steam rose up like tiny ghosts. He started to take his coat off and then pulled it back on. "Christ—it's a little warmer in here than out there, but not by much." He looked at the priest. "Sorry, Father."

Father Marco lifted a hand. "It ain't my name. Ain't me who's offended, but the Lord. But you're right. It is a bit chilly."

"Sorry," Kelsea said. "I guess I got used to it. I thought it was just me, anyways."

James walked over to the thermostat. "You have it set down to fifty."

"Really?" Kelsea shuffled over. He was right. The slider was down just a millimeter south of fifty degrees. "I don't remember adjusting it. Though I guess I've been sleepwalking recently, maybe I did it last night."

James and Father Marco exchanged a look.

"Come on," Kelsea said. "Seriously. I probably did it sleepwalking."

"Or…" James said, "demonic forces. Don't you think, Father?"

"Surely could be just that," Father Marco said, reaching into his bag. He pulled out a small bottle of red wine and some wafers wrapped in a paper towel. "Shall we move to the table?"

They sat around the table. James's lasagna was steaming in the center, and its aroma made Kelsea's mouth water and stomach rumble.

Let's get this over with, she thought.

Father Marco removed his knit cap, revealing a shiny bald pate poking up from short black hair around the sides of his head. "In the name of the Father, the Son, and the Holy Ghost, amen," he said, crossing himself. He paused and looked at them. "Well, Jimmy, I figure it's been a while since you've partaken of the Holy Eucharist, ain't that right?"

James nodded, a little uncomfortable.

"And you, Ms. Hendricks?"

"It's Stone, sir. But um, yes, sir. Father. I can't say I recall having ever, um, partaken."

"Pardon me. Ms. Stone. Anyway, I know this ain't the normal way we might do things, but do y'all got any sins to confess before we begin? 'Tis a frightful thing to partake unworthily. Especially considering your situation here."

An awkward silence passed over them. James looked down at his empty plate. After some time, Kelsea shook her head.

Father Marco sighed. "This might be a long night," he said. "But I can't blame you. I wouldn't want to be airin all my dirty laundry here over the dinner table neither. Might upset the lasagna," he said, and laughed at his joke, much more loudly than Kelsea thought was appropriate for a man of God. "Okay, so I'm gonna try to skip some of the long stuff, just get down to business. May God forgive all of our sins, et cetera."

He poured some of the wine into a glass and laid three wafers on his plate.

"Whoops, nearly forgot," he said. He dug once more into his bag.

Kelsea gave James a look, and he shrugged.

The priest pulled out a larger cracker, a small bottle of water, and a piece of white cloth. He set them all on the table. "Say, Ms. Hendricks—you happen to have a bowl somewhere?"

"Sure," she said. She thought about correcting him about her name again, but decided it wasn't worth it.

She went over to the cabinet and brought back a cereal

bowl. Father Marco set it next to his plate and poured water into it, muttering some prayer below his breath.

This is all so surreal, Kelsea thought, watching the denim-clad priest raising the large cracker and blessing it.

"Blessed are ye, O God of Creation, who have provided this bread in your goodness. We offer it, and by your grace shall it become to us the Bread of Life." He set it down on the table. He paused. When neither James nor Kelsea responded, he whispered, "Blessed be God forever."

"Blessed be God forever," James said. Kelsea responded the same, a bit behind James.

Father Marco raised the glass of wine. "Blessed are ye, O God of Creation, by your goodness we have this wine, it will become our spiritual drink."

Again he paused, and James and Kelsea responded in unison, "Blessed be God forever."

Father Marco bent his head and muttered another prayer as he dipped his hands in the bowl of holy water. He wiped his hands on his cloth, then raised the cracker and said, "And when they were eating, the Lord Jesus took and blessed the bread, and broke it, and said, 'Eat; this is my body, broken for you.'" He broke the cracker and put the pieces on the cloth. He lifted the glass of wine. "And similarly, after supper, Jesus took the wine and gave it to his disciples, saying, 'Drink; this is my blood, poured out for you in forgiveness of sins. Do this in remembrance of me.'" He set the wine glass on the table and looked around.

"Is there something else we're supposed to say?" Kelsea said.

"No. I just thought there'd be a bit more resistance from the dark forces already." He shrugged, then began to recite the Lord's Prayer. Kelsea and James mouthed along with him, though Kelsea didn't know the words very well.

The priest took a wafer off of his plate and looked down. "Lord, I am not worthy, but heal my soul." He consumed the wafer and took a sip of wine from the glass. "All right, now you two come on and partake."

Kelsea and James both received the elements, Kelsea feeling incredibly weird about all of it. If there *was* some sort of demonic thing going on, she wasn't sure this guy was the priest she wanted leading the defense. He just didn't seem, well, *priestly* enough.

"Great," Father Marco said, setting all the leftover stuff to the side. He dipped his hand in the bowl of holy water and sprinkled some on the food. "Just a precaution," he muttered, almost to himself.

Then he looked at James and Kelsea and smiled. "Now let's eat this lasagna before it gets cold!"

You're back.

Don't worry; I was actually hoping you would return. You'll forgive my previous outburst.

Look at them eat. Each uncomfortable, each for a different reason.

I watched them partake of the Holy Communion. It was hard not to laugh, and hard not to rage, at the same time. They act as if I were some lowly underworld scum, to be driven out into a herd of swine.

(And yet the holy man pauses the exorcism for supper? If I were a demon, they would be the pigs.)

I have more right to this house than they ever will. At least, more right than the man.

But I will let them eat in peace, for now.

The minister doesn't always play by his church's strict rules, but at least he is honest in his faith. It is a shame that, in his faith, he believes I'm a devil. I will show him I'm no devil—I am a being of righteousness, not of evil. But I will show him my power.

Is it evil of me to desire blood for my own blood?

It is written about the Lord whom this minister serves that on His return, His robes will be stained with the blood of his enemies, splashed red like the juice of grapes stomped on in pressing wine. Should not a child of God behave like His only begotten Son?

Let them eat. Let them pray to God. He and I have no argument.

Chapter Twelve

"Is there an attic?" Father Marco asked. "Standard procedure is we pray over each room and toss around the holy water. Generally we start in the attic and move down."

"Uh…" Kelsea racked her brain. She couldn't remember seeing any sort of attic access in any of the upstairs rooms. "I don't know. If there is, I don't know how to get to it."

He nodded. "Okay. We'll start upstairs, in a corner of the house, then work our way around and down. If we happen to come upon the attic access, I'll stick my head up there and say a few words."

He pulled three crucifix necklaces out of his bag, donned one, and handed the other two to James and Kelsea. She felt silly about accepting it, but she didn't want to cause any problems, so she put it on.

A strong gust of wind blew against the house and moaned as it swarmed around the outside. The lights flickered, then went out.

"Hey, boy!" the priest said, and James cursed. Kelsea grabbed the cross hanging around her neck on reflex. "Don't panic," Father Marco said. "Could be the devil, but could also be the storm, and it may come back on."

They stayed still in the blackness and waited to see if the power came back, but it didn't. Kelsea realized her fist was still tight around the necklace, and she was glad that none of them could see the red blooming on her face. She loosened her grip but still held the cross between her index finger and thumb despite her self-consciousness.

Can't hurt, in case there is something to all this mumbo jumbo. Besides, nobody can see me.

The soft wavering light of a Zippo sprang up across the room. Father Marco was using the flame's light to look through his bag. "Shoot," he said. "Forgot the flashlights. Either of you got any?"

"I don't think so," Kelsea said.

James said nothing. In the dim light, long shadows flashed on his face. That barely suppressed childlike terror she had seen him wearing at the river was back. He no longer looked like the strong masculine type she had met at the airport a few nights ago.

"All right," Father Marco said, digging a few objects out of the bag and setting them on the table. Kelsea saw that they were small, fat candles. "Got some of these prayer candles," he said. "A-course, we can still use 'em for prayin, but if we don't walk too quickly they'll help us see, too. Two birds with one stone." He handed a lighted candle to each of them. "Ms. Hendricks, will you do us the honor of leading us to the stairs?"

~

They started in a storage room that Kelsea was discouraged to realize she had missed in her cleaning. They crammed themselves between dusty mirrors, paintings of rolling green landscapes, and more taxidermy.

"Hold this, if you would please," Father Marco said, handing his candle to Kelsea. She took it while he turned his water bottle over onto his fingers. He sprinkled the water three times as he said, "In the Name of the Father, and of the Son, and of the Holy Ghost," with a softness and reverence that juxtaposed almost humorously with the cheap commonness of the plastic bottle in his hand. "Saint Michael the Archangel, defend us in battle. Hail Mary, Full of Grace, the Lord is with thee; shelter us in thy bosom as you did the Holy Babe. Father in Heaven, we are powerless against this evil, and we depend on you for our protection and authority."

He waited, as if for demonic resistance or for the Holy Ghost's indwelling, but neither spiritual team acknowledged the priest's incantations. All Kelsea saw were the shadows of stuffed creatures dancing on the walls; all she heard was the screaming storm outside. The priest took the candle back from Kelsea.

"Father Marco," she asked, not meaning to whisper but unable to avoid it. "I don't mean to be rude. But do we have to go through this in every room?"

He shrugged, and his candle's light bounced, threatening to be extinguished from the sudden movement. "We'll sprinkle the holy water in each room and I'll acknowledge the Trinity. At the end of all this, downstairs, I'll have you, as the owner of the house, say a prayer as well. Probably won't call on Mary and the Archangel each time. I don't figure how it can hurt to mention them once in a while, in case they can lend a hand. But the real power don't come from those two."

"Can you really say that you feel any power at all? From…" She looked up, indicating the Big Man Upstairs. "Or from Hell?"

Father Marco looked at her for a moment, then away. "Let's go on to the next room."

They worked down the hall—tonight the floor seemed to creak a lot more than it had before—and followed a similar pattern for each room. Sometimes Father Marco would invoke other saints or angels, but he always named each person of the Trinity as he sprinkled. With each non-eventful blessing, the priest looked both relieved and disappointed.

They finally came to Kelsea's old bedroom.

Father Marco jiggled the handle. "You got a key to this room?"

"I—no, I don't remember locking it."

"Well, the handle won't turn."

The three of them stood looking awkwardly at each other's candles. Kelsea had a thought. "Hold on," she said.

She left them for the room where she had last changed, trying to hurry but then slowing back down each time the flame from her candle waned. She found her jeans from the other day, fished in the pockets, and pulled out the old key she had found taped inside the grandfather clock. She held it up above the candle to get another glimpse of the intricately detailed crown at its end.

"Ow!"

The flame burned her fingers, and she dropped the key. It bounced under the bed. She knelt down too quickly, and the sour smell of a snuffed candle's smoke hit her as the room went totally black. She spilled hot wax all over one of her hands and cried out. The pain was intense but mercifully brief. She heard the two men hustling down the hall to her.

"Kelsea?" she heard James say.

"I'm fine. It's just my candle." She felt along the floor under the bed. Her fingers brushed past something that felt like a ripped playing card, and she pocketed it without thinking. She soon found the key.

The men came to the doorway, their candles sending out missionaries of light. She relit her own candle from theirs, then lifted up the key. "Let's try this," she said.

A flash of suspicion crossed James's face. "Where, uh— that's… Here, I'll take that." He held out an open palm. In the candlelight, his smile looked neither friendly nor safe.

Kelsea took a step back. "I think I can handle it," she said, and put the key in her pocket. James lowered his hand, and the smile stayed on his face, seemingly pasted on.

What are you hiding, James? Kelsea wondered. *And why is it so important right now?*

"All right, then," the priest said. "Let's go back to the room and get 'er done."

They stepped out into the hall—and froze.

In front of them, barely visible in the flickering candlelight, was a small girl in a yellow dress. Darkness concealed her face, but Kelsea was sure it was the girl from the woods.

Father Marco made a few stuttering sounds, then lifted his crucifix. "*Ecce crucis signum, fugiant phantasmata cuncta,*" he said in a hurried whisper.

The girl took a slow step closer.

"*Ecce crucis signum, fugiant phantasmata cuncta,*" he repeated, still hurried, but louder. "Demon, in the name of Jesus Christ, I command you to flee this house!"

Her face still in shadow, the girl spoke. "Why do you call me a demon? I am an agent of the Lord's will."

The girl was next to them in a blink. Kelsea's heart lurched. The temperature drained below zero, and she smelled wet earth. The flames from the candles now illumined the girl's face: the face of the small girl from her dream, the Young Kelsea. But if *this* wasn't a dream—and that was the girl in the woods...?

The girl looked at them each in turn, almost curiously, but with apparent anger. "An eye for an eye," she said. Then with one icy breath, she blew out all of the candles, and they were blind.

Kelsea felt a tiny cold hand grab hers and wrench her down the hall. She prayed desperately that this was still somehow part of that dream from the night before, but now she wasn't all that sure that the night before had been a dream. She wasn't all that sure of anything.

She heard the two men scrambling in the hallway behind her, falling over each other. "Kelsea! Kelsea!" she heard Father Marco cry out, but she was too terrified to speak, and the girl pulled her forward with supernatural strength. Kelsea heard a door open, then she was flung through the doorway.

"You'll be safe in here," said the girl.

Safe from what? Kelsea wanted to say, but the door slammed shut, and the girl was gone.

She felt her way back to the door. The knob would not turn. "Hello?" she said. "Father Marco? James?" No answer. She banged on the door until her fist bruised, but no one came.

In her blindness, her mind painted absent shapes and shades onto the black canvas around her. She crawled on the floor until she felt the dollhouse, confirming what she had strangely dreaded: she was in her childhood bedroom.

She searched frantically around the room, feeling around for a nightlight or light-up toy. She found a plastic box with a lid, opened it, and felt a bunch of musty plush animal toys. Deep at the bottom of this box, her hand closed around a plastic flashlight.

Please work, please work.

She pulled it out and pushed the button, unsure of if she really wanted to see her surroundings or not.

A faint yellow light came from the flashlight. The batteries didn't have much life left in them, but it was enough for her to confirm that she was alone. She went back over to the locked door. The girl

who? what? a demon? me? a dream? am I going insane?

must not have known that Kelsea had the key. She now pulled it from her pocket in triumph.

Do I really want to go out there? But she left me here for a reason. She'll be back.

Yet there was no keyhole. The key wasn't for this door.

In fact, she found no lock anywhere at all. It was held tight by… by what, Kelsea couldn't—or wouldn't—dare to guess.

She put the key back in her pocket and shined the flashlight around the room again. Outside the window, the snow came down with a vengeance. The meteorologists had been right.

Above one of the beds was an attic access door she hadn't noticed before. Maybe if she could get into the attic, there might be a way into another room. She stood on the bed. The trap door was easily within reach, and she pushed up on it. It would not open. She tried reaching in the cracks around the door and pulling it down, but she had no luck with that, either.

Kelsea

She heard her name brush past her ears like a cold breeze, and at first she was sure that in her terrified state she had heard the moaning wind outside and had mistaken it for her name.

Kelsea

But there it came again, coming down from the attic, low and masculine and sad. The voice sounded familiar, it sounded…

Kelsea

It was the voice that had spoken her name over the phone last night.

"Hello?" she said, but then she stopped herself from saying anything further. That voice was either a product of her own insanity, or of whatever supernatural crap was happening. Either way, she didn't want to mess with it.

She sat down on the bed and looked at the other.

Two beds.

Two dresses.

The girl,

who? what? a demon? me? a dream? good God, I am *going insane*

an image of her youth that she had long forgotten.

The dream last night. Either she was still dreaming—and if she was, it was a real doozie, someone must have slipped something into her drink or something—or she was losing her marbles.

Or, as she was still trying to let herself accept, last night was *not* a dream, she was *not* going crazy, and whatever was happening inside this creepy house was *real*.

Her flashlight was weakening. It now emitted less light than had the tiny prayer candle. Before it completely ran out of juice, she got down to the floor and lifted the bedskirt.

The tiny amber circle from the bulb showed the side of a large, green, splintery wooden box.

She dragged it out from under the bed and looked at the lid. The keyhole looked like it would accommodate the key from the clock. A key that seemed to have been purposely hidden. A key that James seemed to covet; a key that he had lied about.

She pulled the key out of her pocket and put it slowly into the lock.

It fit.

She twisted its metal crown.

It turned.

Hesitantly, with an increasing sense of dread, but without being able to help herself, much like last night when she had thought she was dreaming and hadn't been able to resist the journey outside to the shed, she lifted the rough wooden lid.

She shined the flashlight on the box's contents and screamed.

Chapter Thirteen

"Kelsea! Kelsea!" Father Marco shouted, but he heard no answer.

Dear God, don't let her be hurt.

A large hand grabbed his wrist and jerked him down the dark hall, away from the direction in which Marco was sure Kelsea had gone.

"We've got to go after Kelsea!" Marco said.

"We can't help her if that thing gets us first," James said as he pulled the priest. "We need to regroup, strategize."

They entered a room, and Marco heard James shut the door. Marco pulled the lighter from his pocket and relit his prayer candle. He crossed himself and muttered an "In the name of the Father, Son, and Holy Ghost" for good measure, shuddering at that last word. James held his candle out and Marco lit it from his own, then James rested his back against the closed door to catch his breath.

Marco almost jumped out of his skin when he looked around the room. It was the room full of hunting trophies, some of them predatory in their former lives. A black bear lumbered on the other side of the room. A coyote howled up at the ceiling. A slinking bobcat frozen mid-stride stood next to him on a ledge covered in fake moss that jutted out from the wall at eye level. The beasts remained still, but the flames reflected in their glass eyes gave the illusion of voracious souls barely restrained by the deadness of their flesh. The priest prayed that resurrection would not be on the night's list of supernatural phenomena.

"What's going on here?" James asked. "I thought you could handle this stuff. That thing was almost laughing at you."

"You told me this was demonic oppression! That weren't a demon. It was an angry soul, not yet departed to her eternal restin place. Don't know why. Maybe tryin to do somethin about an old grudge. The spirit thinks she is on the side of righteousness, and so she don't shrink back from holy things."

James fumed, but he said nothing.

"Do you know anything about this?" Marco asked.

"No. I have no idea what's going on."

"Think, man. You used to tend to the old Hendricks couple all the time. They didn't say nothin? I only got a quick glimpse of her, but I'll be the Pope's uncle if she didn't look just like their little girl that died. But I don't have a clue why she'd be stickin around after all these years."

"You have to know some way to get rid of her, right?"

Marco tried to calm his beating heart and think. All those potato chips his sister had warned him about were catching up to him at once and making him regret his indulgence, and not the absolving kind. He only drank for communion, and he never smoked or dipped tobacco, and he had only tried marijuana once—and that was back in high school, and he had confessed and repented—but every man had to have a vice, and he figured if grease and cholesterol were to be his undoing, at least he would die a happy man.

But the girl left them no time to draft a new plan. Through the wall next to them she came, with no respect for solid matter. Marco had been afraid of this, though he had hoped that maybe since she seemed to be able to manipulate the physical world—she had been able to blow out the candles, and she had pulled Kelsea away—perhaps she would be bound by its physical laws. Apparently not.

Marco saw his breath and felt beads of cold sweat forming on his bald spot. "Spirit," he said, his voice shaking. "We were mistaken about your nature. I was misinformed."

The girl ignored him and walked over to the opposite wall. She approached a shotgun that was racked on the wall next to a grouse that hung suspended in flight. She took it and pointed it at James.

"Please," Marco said, praying silently that the gun wasn't loaded. "Please. I'm sorry for callin you a devil. Clearly you're—"

"Be quiet," the girl said. She did not take her eyes from James.

Marco looked at the man, who had his hand over his heart as if he had already been shot. James slowly pressed his back flat against the door. It looked like he was trying to melt through the wall like the ghost had done, forgetting, in his terror, the doorknob next to his hip.

"We don't mean you harm," Marco said.

This time the girl looked at him, briefly, and he saw the roiling anger on her face. "Harm has already come to me!" she shouted. "And I've waited for a quarter of a century in this childish form, to repay the harm. To exact justice."

"What's she saying, James?"

James's eyes were wide. Marco saw him take in a breath to answer, but the words got trapped somewhere in his throat, and he only shook his head. Marco heard a sound that he first thought was the rattling of dry bones; then he realized the windows were shaking in their frames.

I should have been a Baptist, he thought. *The Baptists never get called for stuff like this.*

The girl clicked back both hammers on the double-barreled shotgun. Her finger curled around one of the triggers.

He stepped between James and the girl. *This is stupid, Marco,* he told himself. *Don't do this.*

"Get out of my way, holy man; don't interfere with justice. You of all people should know that the Lord is just."

He thought of how strange it was to see the shine of that double-barrel, so solid and heavy, strangely suspended by an immaterial wisp. It was an unnerving sight, looking into the black abyss of the shotgun muzzle and seeing the same black anger on the semitransparent face of a child. He felt his balls seize up. She was no more than five or six years old, but there was an eternity of hate and longing in her that made her seem even older than the twenty-five years she had claimed to have waited between this world and the next.

"Please, don't," he said.

Over the racket of the window glass, from somewhere else in the house, came a woman's scream.

Kelsea, Marco thought.

"You won't stop me," the girl said. "This is what I stayed for, my *destiny*. Get out of my way. That's your last warning."

Both windows shattered inward, spewing glass and letting in swirling winds that extinguished the candles and turned the sweat on the priest's bald spot into frost. Behind him, James swore.

Marco put up his hands. "Says the prophet, 'Come, let us reason together...'" He took a half step in the dark toward the girl.

"*Don't interfere with my—*" the girl screamed, and then in that eternal and instant fragment of time Marco remained alive, he saw the flash of the muzzle and a hint of surprise on the apparition's face as the gun kicked back.

The shot obliterated Father Marco's chest, and what was left of his weight flew back into James, throwing the door open.

~

Brought to his senses by the gunshot, James heaved the priest's deadweight body off of himself, got to his feet, and ran just as another blast put a hole in the floor where he had been. Behind him, he heard the heavy clatter of the shotgun falling to the floor. It was empty, and the girl would have to find new shells to reload, but he didn't feel like giving her too much time for that.

His hand against the wall, he ran until he felt the stairwell's opening, then practically fell down the stairs before sprinting to the front door. Like the room upstairs, it wouldn't open, even when he turned the deadbolt back and forth.

He grabbed the table next to the door and threw it against one of the tall windows. It blew out, and James's hair was blown back with the blizzard winds that came rushing in. He leaped through the open window and pushed his way through the wind to the truck he had loaned to Kelsea.

He pulled a shovel from the truck's bed and frantically dug out the tires and brushed the snow from the windshield. He felt around the wheel well until he found the spare key he kept hidden there; then he hopped in. To his relief, the engine roared to life without much difficulty. He shifted into four-wheel drive and drove out.

He would be back for Kelsea, but not now, when the darkness ruled and the girl had the advantage. But he would be back.

Chapter Fourteen

The door had remained locked the whole night, forcing her to sleep in the same room as—as *that*.

She glanced reluctantly over at the box. She had closed it last night before banging for hours on the door, screaming for James, or Father Marco, or even the girl to let her out. Eventually she had collapsed in exhaustion.

Now she looked out the window at a bleak, gray morning that still spit snow in a swirling torrent.

This kind of nightmare didn't happen in LA. The city was always living, the lights always on, the streets always full—no dark, empty spaces for spirits to claim. Or if there were, she was always too busy to notice, and that was fine with her.

She heard a creak, and looked over at the box again. It was opening.

She froze, half-expecting its contents to rise on their own, like its lid just did, but nothing else happened. Just an open box, beckoning her over for one last look.

And terrified and revolted as she was, she couldn't help but heed its call. She crept toward the green wooden box on hands and knees. As she drew closer, she thought she heard voices whispering from the attic above her.

She again looked down into the box with dread, though she knew full well what lay inside: a child's skeleton in a summer dress, its skull grinning up at her with eye sockets as empty as black holes.

Two beds. Two dresses.

The photograph in the book. The girl had the same face as mine—the same face and yellow dress as the ghost—but the name on the back of the picture... it was different.

Kelsea pulled the card from her pocket, the one she had found under the bed last night before everything got crazy. It was another torn photograph, another little girl who looked just like a young Kelsea. Except this one really *was* her. On its back was her name: *Kelsea.* The younger version of herself held another tiny hand in her own.

This was the final piece to the torn family portrait.

She heard the bedroom door open behind her. She spun, expecting to see the girl, but the doorway was empty.

She stepped out slowly. Immediately she saw a gruesome sight down the hall: a body lying in a pool of blood. Father Marco.

She ran to him. His eyes stared up at the ceiling like a man in a trance, lifeless. The hole in his chest was clotted with dark, dried blood.

Kelsea felt vomit rising and ran to the bathroom. She kneeled over the toilet until everything was expelled. Her stomach ached from the lurching, and her throat burned with acid. She ran water into her hands, slurped it up, and spit it out. It only washed out some of the taste.

From downstairs came the loud and low chime of the grandfather clock. And even though she knew that this should be impossible, that the grandfather clock was no longer here, she did not start at it, was not surprised. She knew it was calling her, and she went.

A frigid breeze blew up the staircase. When she reached the bottom, Kelsea saw that one of the windows by the door had been blown out. But when she stepped that way to investigate, the clock rang again, beckoning her back toward the other room. She obeyed the summons.

In the clock room, the TV was on. It was playing a home video, taken in this very house. Kelsea's parents were in it, and then Kelsea herself... but something wasn't right. The quality was too good. Not grainy, or wavy, like those old VHS films she had watched as a kid in foster care. The picture was sharp and clean, the colors vibrant as real life. Ultra-high definition, but strangely without sound.

On the screen, six-year-old Kelsea lay sick in bed. Her mother, Darlene, bent over her with a thermometer, sticking it under her daughter's tongue. The lines of worry and tender concern on the beautiful woman's face brought a lump to the older Kelsea's throat as she watched the television. She remembered none of this.

Eyes glued to the screen, she sat down to watch.

~

The picture cuts to Miles, downstairs in his office, on the phone with someone, smoke curling up from a pipe in his hand. It's impossible to tell what he's saying; there is no sound.

Cut to the back yard. The sky is clear and deep blue. The grass is green and the trees full. A copy of Kelsea—her twin—swings on the tire hanging from the apple tree. A boy stands next to her, watching and talking. He is young, but older than the small girl: maybe twelve or thirteen.

The girl laughs and hops off the swing. The boy says something, and she makes an ew face.

The boy puts a hand on her shoulder. She takes a step back, confused and a little afraid. He steps toward her; she turns and runs.

An exposed root from the apple tree trips the boy as he chases her, allowing the girl to get a lead. But she is no match for a boy twice her age. He catches up to her before she gets to the woods, and he grabs her.

The girl's expression is one of sheer terror. The boy tries to console her, but it isn't working. He looks around to see if anyone sees them, then he pulls the girl into the forest.

The picture cuts to the riverbank. The boy holds the girl tightly. Tears stream down her reddened cheeks. Bits of sticks and leaves are stuck all through her hair. The boy again tries to quiet her, and the girl screams more.

The boy's face flushes with frustration, and he shakes her. Of course, this does nothing to calm her. For a moment, he takes his hands off of her, and she tries to run again. He grabs the back of her shirt and throws her down. She stumbles into the river, and the current sweeps her downstream.

Cut to the boy, wading somewhere downstream, picking the girl off of the dead tree that has snagged her dress and trapped her underwater. He sloshes back to the bank and sets her down, almost tenderly. He tries some version of CPR, but it is too late. The girl isn't coming back.

Panic rises on the boy's face. He paces back and forth, and keeps glancing down at the girl, as if soon she will awake from her death. He starts to cry, not tears of sorrow as much as fear of being discovered. He stops pacing and stares at the little dead girl for a full minute. Then he runs.

Cut to the shed. The boy rifles through the junk. He finds a green wooden box with a brass crown-shaped key in the lock. He opens the box and leaves it on the floor of the shed.

Cut to the woods, the girl still lying on a bed of wet leaves and moss. The boy running through the woods, stopping at her head. He hooks his hands under her arms and drags her back the way he came. At the edge of the woods, he sticks his head out into the yard to see if anyone is watching. Then he hurries the dead girl into the shed and shuts the door behind him.

Later, the door of the shed opens. The boy, pale-faced and hands shaking, still dripping river water and now also sweat, runs to the back deck. He flings the door open and yells. Even without sound, it is easy to read the words on his lips:

Mr. and Mrs. Hendricks, come quick!

The parents rush to him. The worry on their faces turns to terror, and the three of them run to the river.

But of course, there is no body where the boy takes them.

The river must have washed it away, *he says.*

Cut to the shed. It is twilight now, and the boy creeps inside, but he doesn't dare turn on the light. He pushes the box under a shelf and covers it with tools and scraps of wood.

He leaves the shed and walks toward the edge of the woods. A floodlight comes on, and a weary Mr. Hendricks walks out to see him. The boy is holding something in his fist, and when he sees Mr. Hendricks he tries to shove his hands into his pockets. But the shorts he is wearing have no pockets. He puts his hands behind his back.

Again, there are no words, but the conversation is easy enough to figure out.

What are you doing out here?

I… I…

Come inside, boy. It's getting dark. You won't do anyone any good if you fall in looking for her.

The boy looks at his feet.

You can't blame yourself, Jimmy.

The man leads Jimmy inside. Mrs. Hendricks is on the couch, weeping. She is holding a picture of the girl so tightly that her knuckles are white. Mr. Hendricks puts a hand on her shoulder.

Mrs. Hendricks sees Jimmy and tries to smile. Then she gets up and leaves the room.

Mr. Hendricks hurries down the hall to console his wife. Jimmy starts to go after them, but then spies a roll of tape lying on the table next to the couch. He stops, checks to see that Mr. Hendricks isn't looking, then tears off a strip of tape and presses it to the item in his hand: the key to the green box. He sticks it inside the grandfather clock, then hurries after Mr. Hendricks.

⁓

The TV turned itself off. Kelsea wondered whether it had actually been on.

She felt a presence. She turned and saw the girl standing next to the sofa.

"Kayla?" Kelsea said. "You were my sister?"

The girl nodded.

"And... the boy... that was James?"

Hate blackened the girl's face, and she nodded again. "Now you know why I'm still here."

Kelsea's anger and sorrow over what she had seen were starting to outweigh her fear and disbelief. The room seemed to spin around her. *James killed this girl?* The idea that she had toyed with romantic feelings for that monster sickened her. She wondered how much danger she had been in keeping his company.

But she might still be in danger; she wasn't convinced she was out of the angry ghost's sights.

"Did you kill the sheriff?" she asked the girl.

"His death is on his own head. The police were so quick to believe Jimmy's story. No investigation. Not even suspicion."

"But that was a long time ago. Was this sheriff even there back then?"

The girl shrugged. "Who cares? They're all the same. Besides, time doesn't pass the same to me in this form. The day I was killed was centuries ago; the day I was killed was yesterday. All feels like eternity."

"But what about Father Marco? Did you kill him too?"

The girl looked away for a second, and even her pale deathly face seemed to blush the slightest pink. She tightened her lips. "He got in my way! I'm only a minister of justice. If he was foolish enough to come between me and my ministry, then he deserved what happened to him."

Kelsea shrank back some. She looked down at her lap. "Are you going to hurt me, too?"

Kayla sat next to her and placed a small, freezing hand on her arm. "I was jealous of your life when I first saw you, but not anymore. I'll be satisfied when I take care of the man. How could I harm you? You're family."

"Some family," Kelsea said, almost to herself. "Our parents hated me, and now I find I have a sister who haunts my house."

"Mom and Dad never hated you; they loved you. But after they lost me, they were buried in grief. Mom had a nervous breakdown. Since you and I shared the same face, Mom couldn't look at you without seeing me. Only a month later, I found her in the bathtub, cutting her wrists."

"Oh God."

"I was trying to stop the bleeding when you walked in. Dad heard you screaming, and I left before he arrived. He was able to save her, just barely. You remember none of this?"

Sickening, horrifying images flashed through Kelsea's mind, and reflexively she tried to shake them out. Terror and sorrow rose from some long-forgotten, dark aquifer in her soul. She couldn't speak.

Kayla continued. "Mom and Dad were private people, but word got around. After 'the accident' of my death, and then Mom's suicide attempt, it wasn't long before the state swooped down and snatched you away."

"So…" Kelsea's words caught in her throat. "I always thought they put me up for adoption themselves."

"No. They said Mom was too unstable, too dangerous for you to be around."

"They never tried to see me again," Kelsea said. It still felt to her as if her parents had thrown her away. "If they loved me, why didn't they try to contact me?"

"Dad was at his wits' end with Mom. She got better, but she never recovered fully. They both became reclusive. Mom hardly ate. Dad eventually lost his businesses. He blamed himself for everything. Didn't think he deserved to have you back; figured you would resent him for not fighting the state harder."

Kelsea wasn't sure how to feel. On the one hand, she felt guilty for her misplaced anger toward Miles and Darlene. On the other hand, she still couldn't accept that they had never even tried to speak to her again. Resentment was a hard emotion to drop so quickly. The conflicting feelings swirled within her like the snowstorm outside.

"Somehow they kept going on what they had saved, but neither of them was ever the same," Kayla said. "It was hard for me to watch—even harder to see that they still loved the one who destroyed me. They treated him like a son." Kelsea felt a cold puff of air pass her face as Kayla spat the word *son* with malice.

"What happened to James last night? Did you…"

Kayla sighed. "He got away. He took the truck he loaned you. He is likely back at his house, nursing his wounds. Which is unfortunate, as I am bound to this property alone until my task is completed. But he'll be back."

"What makes you so sure? If he knows that you're trying to kill him, won't he just leave the house alone?"

"He can't. He's been plagued with guilt and paranoia ever since he met you. Why do you think he never mentioned me? He will have to assume that by now you've learned what he did."

"What do you mean?" Kelsea said.

"He will not risk his secret getting out," Kayla said. "He'll have to come back to kill you. And when he does, I will be ready."

She asked if she could be alone. I left her to think. I fear she'll try to leave the house, to escape both me and the man. She won't be able to, though. She doesn't have keys to the vehicles outside. And even if she did, she knows she lacks the ability to drive in this weather. The plows cannot keep up with this storm.

And I can't let her. Her presence in this house ensures that the man will be back. And she won't be safe until I have my vengeance—who knows to what lengths he will go to track her down and kill her for his secret?

Maybe I should take some steps to ensure what must come, and to prevent the man's escaping in a similar way.

I wonder if it will be today. Will he rush back to finish her? Or will he wait, strategize?

I admit that I am nervous, now that I have lost the element of surprise. I wonder if killing the priest was necessary. I also admit that my finger slipped, and the gun went off before I meant it to. But I would be lying if I told you that I would not have shot him in the next two seconds, had my finger not chosen to do so when it did.

But he still got away, and if I had not spent that extra shell, perhaps I could have killed him as he shoveled out his truck.

It hardly matters now. As long as she stays, I'm certain he'll be back. And where can she go?

Look at my hands. They are spirit, not the weak flesh they used to be, but still they tremble when I think of what is to come.

Chapter Fifteen

Faith rocked back and forth in her favorite chair as she sipped her coffee.

"I know you been up to somethin, honey," she said to her empty living room. "I seen the Jeep comin and goin the past few days."

Her chair creaked and made soft rubbing sounds against the carpet.

"Why ain't you talkin to me, dear?"

Faith had been awake since the dark of five. These days, she usually found herself unable to sleep past four or five, whether or not she wanted to be up. So it had become her habit to set her coffee pot to start at four thirty, and at least the harsh chill and darkness of the early winter mornings were softened by the warm aroma of fresh brewed coffee when she woke. She would sit in her chair with a blanket on her lap and drink a full pot while she watched the sun rise through the window. Sometimes she sat in that chair until noon. Sometimes she brewed another pot, sometimes she didn't. Always she sat there and chatted with her deceased husband.

Faith's husband had died ten years ago, from a brain tumor. "Faith," he had said weakly on his hospital bed, "I know I oughta be jumpin to see my Savior and live with Him in glory." She put a hand on his scruffy cheek, and he held it. "But I ain't ready to rid myself of these holy hills He's made for us." A tear came down and wet their intertwined fingers.

The next day he died.

But he never left. Faith knew his soul couldn't quite give up these mountains, no matter how great the prospect of a mansion in glory. So she would see him from time to time, and they would talk. At other times, she believed he was roaming some other part of Tucker County. Once in a while she heard rumors of someone catching a glimpse of him at a high school football game down in Parsons, or spying him fishing out at Red Creek, or even seeing him passing the window of the Purple Fiddle while a band was playing. Faith noticed his old vehicle (which she hadn't driven herself since he had died) come and go every so often. And a couple times a month he would be there in the living room when she woke up, sitting in his ratty old recliner, and they would either talk or they would sit in silence and enjoy each other's company.

She had been sixteen and beautiful and living on the wrong side of the train tracks down in Augustus Valley when they met. He had been eighteen and muscular and visiting a cousin in the area. She was lying out on a rock near the bridge that summer when he and his cousin came ambling down to the river with their fishing poles. The cousin had given her a glare of a kind she was all too familiar with, but he had walked right up to her and greeted her with a warm smile. He was obviously taken with her, and didn't share his cousin's aversion to the darker race. They met at the river every evening the rest of that week to watch the sun go down. On the last evening, he kissed her and told her he loved her.

They kept in touch, and the next year they were married—much to the chagrin of both families—and the first time she ever left southern West Virginia was the day she moved north to Tucker County. She soon got the impression that the folks in Davis and Thomas had not seen many black people before, and as she had expected, few of them seemed okay with the marriage of one of their beloved sons to this dark-skinned girl from the southern coal fields. But he never gave a rat's ass about their opinions, and though there were certainly times when she resented him for keeping her here in the whitest place in the United States, she never thought of leaving him. God help her, she loved him with her whole heart.

Over time, the people came to accept their marriage as just another oddity to gossip about, *that mixed couple* that lived in Canaan Heights. And eventually even that topic became boring to most of the people.

Faith had even made friends here. People did change, and to their credit, the people of Davis and Thomas had all come to know her by her first name (instead of *the butcher's colored wife*), and most of them smiled and waved when she drove through town. After her husband died, the folks in her church had comforted and supported her through her grief. But even after all this, she had never felt like part of the community. She was something known but still something *other*, a step-cousin to this exclusive, tight-knit family that was the people of the Allegheny Highlands.

She understood why he stuck around here after he died. His love for these hills was even greater than his love for her. That didn't bother her, for he had treated her with the greatest, most tender affection and respect, and had always defended her when the whole world was against them. She had always the sense that she was the only woman in his life, his queen. But she knew that Tucker County was his greatest love.

But why didn't *she* leave? Why not go back down south to Augustus Valley, where she had grown up?

She couldn't leave because, well, he hadn't left, either. As long as he was tethered to these hills and hollers, so was she. When he moved on, so then would she.

And so she rocked every morning and talked to him, and sometimes he was there to talk back.

The white stuff fell from the sky something fierce today, and had been doing so since last night. "Looks like we're stuck in for another big one, honey," she said as she looked out the window and rocked.

A spring in the old recliner squeaked. She turned to see her husband sitting in his chair. He was leaning forward, his elbows on his huge thighs, his chin resting on his hands. He had a serious look on his face.

"Hey, honey," she said. "What's the matter?"

"She's in trouble," he said. "The Hendricks girl is back. It's all happening now."

"What are you sayin, honey? You been tellin me about that Hendricks girl ever since you been... you know. Roamin around on the wind and whatnot."

"No, the other one. The one they took away. She's back, and she's in trouble. You gotta help her. She don't trust me, but maybe she'll trust you. Jimmy will be back for her any time now. She's stuck in the house, nowhere to go."

"What do you want me to do?" Faith looked out the window again. The snow was still falling heavily, and she knew the plows had quite a ways to go to catch up with it. "I'm about as stuck in as she."

"I don't know, but we gotta do somethin. That boy ain't right, you know it, and what he done all them years ago is comin back to him. I warrant he'll do about anything to cover it all back up. Including killing that girl. You still got the old skis, right?"

Faith paused, then nodded slowly. They had both bought cross-country skis when they married, in hopes of staying in shape. They made use of them all of two winters before the skis and boots got shoved back to some forgotten corner of the house, never to be seen or thought of again—until now. "I can find the skis. But I don't know how well I'd get there, cold rattly bones I got now, and muscles like jelly."

"I know. But I don't know what else to do. I'm sure Jimmy will go back. And besides all that, there's a lot going on at that house, souls being bound in ways they shouldn't and all."

"Bound souls; you don't say, hon. When *you* gonna go on and get outta here? I ain't keepin you, am I?"

She almost wanted him to say yes, that any Heaven would be Hell without her, but she knew—yes, she knew, and she didn't have to think it, and he didn't have to say it, and it was still all right, she knew the love that was between them even now, even if his love for the mountains was greater. And so he said nothing, and she nodded in reply to all that was unsaid.

"You're right, though," she said. "I'll go. Even if just to give the girl company if trouble comes." She laughed. "And we both know I'm too old and lonely to care much about what life I got left. Tell me this though: this other Hendricks girl, is she worth it?"

He shrugged, and then he nodded. "She ain't a bad woman. She don't deserve no harm to come to her. She still don't know this place as her home or love it any, but you can't blame her for it. She's just now finding out where she came from. She's one of our own, got these country roads deep in her blood."

Faith stood. She rubbed a sore spot in her back, and stretched. "All right. I'll find the skis."

"And bring my old .45. You know where it is."

Faith nodded. Her husband stood and walked to the door.

"You ain't gonna come with me?" she said.

"I told you, Faith. She don't trust me. I don't reckon I'd be of any help. I'll see you again."

"You promise?"

"Of course, dear. You know I love you." He took a breath (or did he? she often wondered whether ghosts really needed the air, or if they just breathed for show), and then he said, "You know how I am, and it is what it is. But West Virginia ain't all that holds me back, you know. I do love you and miss you."

Faith's old heart broke, and she smiled. "I love you too, Russ."

He walked through the front door. Faith—or Widow Pifer, as most folks now called her—looked out the window and watched Russ's figure disappear into the snow. Then she went to look for the skis.

Chapter Sixteen

Kelsea stared at the ceiling, her feet hanging off the edge of what had been either her or her sister's old bed. A knocking sound came from downstairs, but Kelsea was too distracted by her thoughts to pay it any attention.

My sister.

She still couldn't believe it. After all that had happened, all that was happening now—a haunted house and people killed and James a murderer—the thing that was the hardest for her to process was that she had a twin sister. A sister she had lost in a dark closet in her subconscious where her childhood memories had been locked away.

And now here she was, reunited with her in absolutely the most unusual way possible. Yet the girl was unbalanced, angry, and out for blood. But who could blame her? She had been abused and then murdered by someone she had thought was a friend. And at such a young age! Trauma like that could ruin a person for the rest of their life. Kelsea had never imagined how something like that might affect a person's *after*life—not that she had really believed in one until now.

Kelsea was still hurt and angry with Miles and Darlene for cutting her out of their lives completely. Now, she sort of understood why, if she hadn't yet forgiven them for it. She was the living image of their lost daughter. No wonder there were rumors about them going crazy; in some ways, they probably had—her mother, at least.

"Why didn't you reach out?" she groaned. "Why would you keep me out of your lives?"

Again the picture came to her mind of her mother, naked and bleeding in the bathtub. She squeezed her head in her hands.

This can't be. This just doesn't happen to people. It just isn't... I'm crazy. I'm going crazy.

She didn't want to accept that this was an actual memory, so traumatic to her young psyche that she had repressed it all these years.

She thought back on all the pictures she had found around the house, how in every one of them after that incident there wasn't an ounce of joy to be found on their faces.

And what about James? She could hardly believe what she had seen. But it must be true; why would the girl

Kayla, her name is Kayla; she's my sister—how do I have a sister?

lie about it? Why else would she be hanging around?

Kelsea

Again, the voice from the attic.

"Who's there?" Kelsea said to the ceiling. Once again, she stood up on the bed and tried to pry the door open, but it wouldn't give. She lay back down on the bed.

Being in the same house as her dead sister (both in spirit and physical remains, Kelsea realized as she looked at the closed green box) was hard enough to come to terms with. This voice she kept hearing... Maybe she *was* going insane. And if the voice wasn't real, who was to say any of this was?

No. She couldn't be crazy. As surreal as this whole experience was, it was strangely restoring the pieces of her that, deep down, she had always known were missing, filling in the gaps within her soul that she had always ignored.

Kelsea

But if she wasn't crazy, then to whom did the whispers from the attic belong?

Chapter Seventeen

It took Faith an hour to find the skis and wrangle them out of the back of the closet. *You could have at least helped me get these old things out, Russ.* But now they were laid out on her living room floor, and she was dressed and ready to go.

She took a long look out the window at the blizzard. It looked cold out there. The reality of the danger she might face at the house had not quite hit her, but she sure felt hesitation at the idea of going out into the storm, when her house was so warm and peaceful.

"You can't live in a better place," Russ had told her once. "Ain't no disasters here that can really bring you down. No twisters, no hurricanes, no earthquakes. Not even forest fires—it's too wet, generally speaking. It flooded once back in eighty-five, but that ain't likely to happen again, and our place is too high up to get much of that. No, all we get is a couple bad blizzards every winter, and all you gotta do is hunker down for a week or two. As long as you got food and your gas stays on and your power don't go out, you'll be fine, cozy as all get-out."

But now Faith was about to leave her cozy-as-all-get-out home and go out in the one kind of weather that could possibly do a bit of harm to a rusty old widow like herself. And then what? Stop a man half her age from killing some girl she didn't know?

One thing at a time, Faith old girl, she told herself. *Can't sit around when a body needs help. Especially if it's so important to Russ.*

She hefted the skis and poles into a bundle and trudged outside. The snow was up to her waist straight out the door, and drifted higher in some parts. She felt the tips of her flat old breasts harden up from the cold, and oddly, this made her chuckle.

Both Russ's Jeep and her old Lincoln were quickly being erased by the snow. Her heart fell. She had hoped to drive the Jeep at least part of the way before using the skis. But it looked like she wouldn't even be able to get out of the driveway. Even if she could, she sure wasn't going to be able to get down the steep road to the valley without hitting a pine or two and ending up having to hire someone to tow the thing out of the woods whenever spring rolled around.

She picked her way through the lower sections of the snow. Twenty years ago she might have been able to ski down the mountain, but not now. She would have to walk slowly down to the valley, staying to the side of the road and close to the trees, where the snow was shallower and she could hold on to the branches. Then she would put on the skis. It ought to be flat enough all the way to the Hendricks's place that she could ski without losing control and breaking a hip or blowing out a knee.

She had quite a trek ahead of her.

She carried her skis to the edge of the driveway where the road began to descend. She set the skis down and let them slide as far as they would go themselves. Then, using the poles to brace herself, she walked, her joints creaking, Russ's gun in her coat pocket slapping against her side. The cold metal's weight somehow made it seem sentient.

"Russ," she said between deep breaths, "if you weren't dead already, I'd kill you myself. *Lordy*!"

Chapter Eighteen

James woke late in the morning. His mouth and throat were sore and cotton-dry, and his body ached from last night's craziness and a fitful, restless sleep. He didn't want to get out of bed. But he had a job to finish.

He groaned, pushed himself up, and walked to the bathroom. He poured a glass of water from the faucet, drank it down, then splashed cold water on his face. Red eyes in deep, baggy sockets stared back at him from the mirror. His beard was getting out of control, just like this whole mess.

He put his elbows on the sink and leaned his face into his hands. He couldn't risk Kelsea getting away now. It was a crying shame; it really was. At first, when he had sensed her attraction to him, he had decided to pursue that avenue in order to gain her trust and keep her from finding out about Kayla. But it had become more than strategy; he had *liked* her, had really hoped for some action—maybe even a real relationship. That would have been hard with her living in LA, but then again, distance had its advantages, too.

All that was ruined now. She had seen the girl. And

whether or not the runt had told her anything, it wouldn't be long before Kelsea put the pieces together herself. Especially now that she had that key.

He should have gotten rid of that dusty old box when he'd had the chance. But he had never been able to bring himself to take it while the old man and woman were still kicking. He was afraid they would see him, afraid of the questions they might ask. And as long as neither Miles nor Darlene was going out to the shed themselves—and they never did, never did much of *anything* since the girl died—James's secret was as safe out there as anywhere.

When the couple was out of the picture, though, James did try to move the box—once. But when he opened the shed's door and saw the girl's silhouette back there, beside the box, he turned tail and hadn't set foot in the shed since—avoided the entire property as much as possible until the sister came to town. The one time he did return, to tame that jungle of a lawn, he brought his own mower, too scared to go into that old pile of boards where he knew the girl waited for him.

But the girl hadn't just waited in the shed. She was in the house, now.

And instead of one girl problem, now he had two.

It was possible, he thought, that the girl had killed Kelsea herself. The ghost hadn't seemed emotionally stable last night. But he would have to go back, to be sure. And soon. First Coop, and now the priest was dead. It would only be so long before people came looking.

This storm was a blessing in that way: no way was

anybody driving through Canaan Valley for a while. That bought him a bit of time—but not much. He had to go back and finish this whole business today.

He ran some water through his hair and did his best to make it look presentable. He didn't want to look like a psychopath on the off chance that Kelsea was still unaware of his part in all this. If he still had her trust, it would make his job all the easier.

He still had to figure out how to keep away from the girl, though.

Thanks for nothing, Father Marco—what a disaster. Want something done right, gotta do it yourself, as they say. What to do, what to do?

An idea came to him. A memory of his grandmother, rocking on her chair in front of the fire, dark shadows dancing across her face like demons as her scratchy-throated voice told tall tales of ghouls and warlocks and trolls, spells that cast goose pimples over his skin.

Salt 'n' sage, Jim-boy. That's how you do it. You ever come crost a haint that don't play nice, all you need is a shaker o' salt 'n' some burnin sage, and they's nothin that haint can do to you no more.

It was nothing more than superstition, James had always thought. None of Granny's old charms and potions and incantations had kept the cancer from eating out her lungs. Then again, he *was* dealing with the stuff of superstition here. And it was the best he had to go on, now that the useless priest was gone.

He looked through his cupboard until he found a bundle

of dried sage. He had thought he had bought it for cooking, but maybe Granny had been there in the back of his mind all along, telling him, *Say, Jim-boy, you reckon you should have some o' that sage on hand? Ain't no tellin when an ol' angry haint might come crost your path. Might well be sooner than later, with what you done them years ago.*

He put the sage in his coat, along with a shaker of salt.

It can't be this simple. Should have brought this stuff with me last night.

He ate a bowl of cereal and downed a shot of espresso, both of which did wonders for his strength and attitude. By the time he had found his hunting knife and hid it inside his coat with the rest of his stuff, he was actually looking forward to his task. He whistled the tune from that old Steve McQueen movie, *The Great Escape*, as he stepped outside and strapped on his snowshoes.

Chapter Nineteen

Kelsea left the bedroom. "Kayla?"

The only response was that constant knocking and banging below.

The priest's body was gone; apparently Kayla had disposed of it in some way. There was still a lot of dried blood on the floor.

I'm going to have to make sure I get all the blood cleaned up if I'm going to sell or rent this place, Kelsea thought, then realized how bizarre that thought was. She had a lot bigger and more immediate problems than making this place presentable. Like surviving, for instance. She felt like her stomach was filling with lead.

James is a killer.

And Kayla was right: he would be back. Not to save her from the ghost; that had never been his plan. She wondered if he had actually thought Father Marco could have convinced Kayla to leave. Like Kelsea, the poor priest had probably had no idea what he had been dragged into. And now he was dead.

Kelsea wondered how long she would last. Sure, Kayla

seemed to be on Kelsea's side for now—but she didn't seem altogether stable, and Kelsea wondered how much she could trust a bloodthirsty ghost, twin sister or not.

She descended the stairs and found the hallway a lot darker than she had expected. The windows in the living room were covered in crooked, hastily applied slats that let in sparse planes of gray light.

She followed the banging sound to the study. Kayla floated above a pile of old boards by the window. She had a hammer in one hand, a board in the other, and about fifteen nails sticking out from her lips.

The ghost turned and looked down at Kelsea. "He won't get away," she said. Her lips stayed pressed around the nails, but Kelsea still heard her voice clearly. "Once he comes, I can't let him get away again."

"What if I want to leave?"

Kayla's face firmed up, and she turned back to the window and resumed her work.

"Hey! I asked you a question!" Kelsea said. She was trying to sound firm and bold, but her heart was skipping beats.

The girl nailed the board to the window frame with surprising efficiency. Had not Kelsea been frightened for her life, this image of a six-year-old girl floating in the air and wielding a hammer with the strength and dexterity of an experienced carpenter might have been humorous to her.

I can't let her control me, she thought, *but I what if I set her off?*

"Kayla," she tried again, doing her best to sound sweet. "Sister."

Kayla turned, her expression now a bit softer.

"I want to leave, sister. I don't want to stay. You're using me as bait for your trap. You know that isn't right."

"You can't leave," Kayla said, her mouth still closed around the nails. "I need you, sister. I won't fail. I won't let him hurt you."

"I don't want to be part of this."

"That's out of your control now. You have no choice."

Kelsea fought back tears. The girl was right. There was nowhere to run, anyway. Her only choice now was to go along with Kayla's plan.

Kayla seemed to sense Kelsea's surrender. She turned back to her work.

"Kayla, what are… I've been hearing a voice. What's up in the attic?"

Kayla snapped her head back to Kelsea. "Stay out of there!" she said, this time with her lips, and the nails fell out of her mouth and jangled on the floor. Kayla descended to pick up the nails and tried to regain her composure. "Don't worry about that. It's just… something I had to take care of. Temporarily."

"You're scaring me, you know."

The nails back in her mouth, Kayla again spoke with a still face. "I'm a ghost. I scare people. What did you expect?" She again turned to the window. "I have made sure that you can't get into the attic for now. But in any case, stay away. I have waited too long for this time to come, and I cannot afford any distractions. Now, I have work to do, and it is in your best interest to help me. There's another hammer and a box of nails there on the floor."

Kelsea stared. *Is this really happening?*

She sighed. She was still terrified, but it would be better to feel like she was doing something useful rather than just letting circumstances blow her back and forth like a dead leaf falling in the wind. She picked up the hammer, grabbed a few nails, and got to work.

Chapter Twenty

It took Faith much longer than she had expected to reach the junction of Canaan Heights Road and Route 32 down in the valley. Her back and knees hurt. She was sweating under her coat and cursing under her breath.

"Oh, honey," she said. The wind froze the sweat and snow that had accumulated in her short curly gray hair. She took a few great breaths and put a hand on her chest. "Oh, honey, I can't go on."

But as she looked back at her deep tracks up the steep mountain, she knew she had gone too far to turn back now. As hard as the six miles of skiing would be, walking back up the hill in her current state would be even worse. And would Russ forgive her? Of course he would, but the thought of seeing the disappointment on his face was too much to bear.

She found one of her skis near a tree off the side of the road, and another had glided to where the yellow line would show if it weren't buried underneath the snow. She gathered them and tried to step in. She fell a few times, but eventually she felt her boots click into the bindings. She stood, a little wobbly, and sank half a foot down in powder.

"Here we go," she said. She started down the long white road.

Chapter Twenty-One

They didn't have any boards big enough to seal the French doors in the back, so Kayla and Kelsea decided to just board up the backs of both lower hallways. They finished this and the rest of the windows downstairs that might provide easy escape. The whole first floor was now dark and gloomy.

"We don't have much wood left," Kelsea said. "Are we doing the upstairs, too?"

"The lower level is the most important," Kayla said, "but we should do what we can with what time we have left."

They moved upstairs. Kelsea had just started to feel more comfortable around her sister's spirit, but the priest's dried blood on the hallway floor made her stomach seize up.

"I told you," Kayla said, "you have nothing to fear from me. Only him."

Kelsea wondered if the girl had read her mind or merely her face.

Kayla floated over the blood and into the room with the hunting trophies. Kelsea stepped carefully around the blood as she followed.

The windows in this room were shattered, and glass littered the floor. Kelsea wrapped her arms tightly around herself to ward off the chill. She didn't ask what had happened in here, just set to work.

"Kayla, did your parents—our parents—did you, uh…"

"I tried to keep out of sight while they were here. I suspected that if they knew I was still waiting around, it would be harder for them to move on. It didn't matter much, I suppose."

Kelsea spoke between her hammering. "What were they like? I don't remember them."

"They were beautiful and loving and happy. Mommy made us clothes and cooked the best pies and pepperoni rolls. Daddy had started a few businesses in Morgantown during college, and then in Thomas a few years before they had us. He had some success early on, despite his youth. He wrote on the side. Poetry was his true love."

"I read one. It was about you."

Kayla shook her head. "It could have been about either of us."

Kelsea made no comment.

"He was a very good writer. But nobody can live on poetry. Fortunately he had his businesses. He had given them such a strong start that they still managed to bring in money for a while even after he had lost his ability to lead them. You can't imagine how sad it was to watch them grow so old and melancholy so quickly."

Kelsea sniffed and hammered the nails a bit harder than she needed to.

They both worked without speaking for a while.

"They never told me anything," Kelsea said finally. "Never tried to find me again. I never knew any of this until now."

"Like I said: they thought you would either resent them or be ashamed. Or both."

"If I resent them now, it's only because they never talked to me after it all. That *was* their fault. I wouldn't have hated them for the rest."

"Maybe that's true. Maybe it's not."

Kelsea ignored her sister's lack of confidence in her. "Were they at peace when they died? James said he found them together."

A ray of light from the window flashed in Kayla's angry eyes as she put up the last board. The room was dark, and Kelsea couldn't see anything but animal shadows from the taxidermy, but she heard Kayla hammer the final nail, and then she heard her say in a low voice, "He found them, all right. But they weren't dead when he entered the house. He stuck a needle in them to make it look like they died naturally. Those incompetent police asked no questions."

"What?"

"You're surprised?"

"It doesn't make sense," Kelsea said. She was about to ask why James had done this when someone called her name from outside.

"He's here," Kayla whispered.

Chapter Twenty-Two

James paused when he saw the boarded-up windows. If he entered and the girl again locked the door, it would be much harder to escape this time. Maybe impossible.

But if Kelsea was still ignorant of his intentions—and on the trek over, he had grown more confident that this was the case—he might be able to lure her out here where the girl had less advantage.

He cupped his hands over his mouth and called out: "Kelsea! Kelsea!"

He waited a minute, but there was no sign of the living twin.

Of course: the girl is keeping her inside, using her as bait. That little shit.

He stepped onto the deck and removed his snowshoes. He peered in through the tiny window in the front door. The living room was dark and empty. No Kelsea. But no ghost, either.

Maybe the girl killed Kelsea in one of her fits.

But he couldn't leave without knowing. He opened the door quietly and crept inside.

"Kelsea?" he whispered.

The living room was warmer than the outside, but not by much. James left the door open in case he needed to make a quick getaway.

He whispered again, a bit more loudly. "Kelsea! Are you here? I've come to help you."

"James!" Kelsea's voice came from somewhere upstairs. "James, she won't let me leave!"

He started for the stairs. "I'm coming!" he whispered. "Where are you?"

He heard a sardonic laugh behind him. The hairs on his neck stiffened. He looked behind him and saw the little girl with three kitchen knives in her hands. She raised a fist and threw two of them. He dove to the side, into a downstairs bedroom, just in time. One knife flew down the hall, and one stuck with a thud in the doorframe.

Lying on the floor of the bedroom, he reached into his coat pocket, pulled out the bundle of sage, and lit the end with his cigarette lighter. It flamed up in the dim room, and he waved it around until the herbs went down to a smoking glow.

If this doesn't work, I'm screwed. Granny, don't fail me now.

The girl appeared in the doorway with a chef knife still in her hand. It was hard to make out her face in the tiny amount of light squeaking through the boards, but he thought he saw her smiling as she walked toward him on weightless bare feet.

He held the smoldering sage in front of him with one

hand and crab-walked backward until he bumped into the wall. The girl neared steadily. A narrow beam of light glinted on the knife's blade.

"Get back!" James said, brandishing the sage.

The girl still smiled cruelly. "After all these eternal, instant years," she said, raising the knife. "Providence now brings you back to me."

No. Not like this. He waved the sage without conviction. His hands trembled. He was sweating. *It's not working.*

Then the girl stopped. Confusion crossed her face, and then anger was added to it. Black tears started to leak out of her eyes, and she put an arm over them.

"What are you doing?" she shouted. "What is this?"

He laughed, surprised that this was actually working. He stood up and sidestepped around the girl, surrounding her with the smoke. She kept one arm over her eyes and waved the other arm blindly, trying to dissipate the offending vapors. She threw the knife, but James easily dodged it.

"Stop it!" she screamed. She coughed and removed her arm from her eyes to see where he was. Thick black ooze was smeared all over her arm and face.

James set the smoking sage down at his feet and pulled the salt from his coat. He shook some out onto his hand and tossed it at her to see what would happen.

The girl jerked back as if in pain.

James laughed. After all the chaos of last night, all he had ever needed was some stuff from the kitchen.

He unscrewed the salt shaker's metal cap and again circled the girl, leaving a thick line of salt surrounding her.

"Sayonara, sister," he said. He dropped the empty salt shaker on the floor and turned away. He put the remains of the sage, which were no longer burning, back inside his coat.

"*No!*" the girl screamed. "Not now!"

James chuckled and shut the door behind him, muffling the girl's angry cries.

"Kelsea, I got her," he said into the empty hall. "We're safe now. Where are you?"

Chapter Twenty-Three

Faith pushed and glided, pushed and glided down the road. Her legs burned, her lungs screamed for more oxygen, her heart thundered within her chest. She felt lightheaded. The only thing she felt good about right now was her pace; she was proud of herself for how quickly she had picked up a good smooth rhythm.

Dear God, help that Hendricks girl, she prayed. *And help me.*

She figured she had done maybe a mile and a half since she got onto the main road, but there wasn't any way to know for sure. Everything was just a blur of white. The only navigational aids she had were the trees on either side, and even those were hard to see through the storm.

At least the wind's at my back. Ain't no way I'd be moving against it.

The road started to decline, long and sweet and not too sharply. She let her legs rest a little. But she knew this was just a dip and she would have to go back up soon, so she pushed off a bit more, trying to build up some momentum to keep her going when the incline started. She picked up speed, now faster than she was comfortable with.

Comfort be damned. Ain't been comfortable since I left the house. Why worry now?

But before the bottom of the dip, she hit an uneven lump in the snow, and it threw her off balance. She let out a cry and tumbled off the road into a deep snowdrift.

She wasn't hurt. The snow was dreamily soft. She took long deep breaths as she lay there. She was sweaty but still warm from all the exertion, and lying down in that fluffy bed felt like heaven.

I might just stay a while. I could sleep here 'til I wake up in glory.

The wind whistled over the pocket her fall had made in the drift. She watched the snowflakes pass across the solid gray backdrop of the winter sky.

Them must be the angels singin and comin to take me away.

She smiled and closed her eyes. "I'm comin to you, Russ, honey."

"Faith."

She opened her eyes. Russ was standing over her.

"Get up. Kelsea needs you."

"But I'm so tired, honey. And there's so much road left. I'll never make it."

"Please try, dear. It ain't your time yet. This ain't the way you want to go."

She sighed. "But it feels so nice. Why can't I just let my soul free right here? Maybe I can help her better if I'm like you."

Russ shook his head, slowly and sadly. His eyes were wet. "It don't always work the same way for everyone. Say that good Death Angel comes to guide you on home, and you say like I did, 'Please, messenger, let my soul tarry for a bit.' And it says back, 'Your mortal body can no longer hold your immortal soul. God sent me to take you away, to be at His side.' And then you say, 'But can't I just wander for a bit more? Can He just send for me by-and-by?'"

"Yes," Faith said. "Tell the Good Lord to send for me by-and-by."

"No!" Russ said, with an intensity that startled her. "No. He may say 'Very well,' but he may not. Or he may say you are bound on earth to such-and-such a place until such-and-such a time. I'm more free to roam than most, but I'm still bound to Tucker County, the treasure of my heart. I know you don't love this place like I do. Who knows what the Lord's messenger might say?"

He turned his head as if he had heard something. Faith, still wavering in resolve and consciousness, heard nothing but the wind.

"Now," Russ said. "Get up. There's a man comin now. He can help you."

He held out his hand.

Faith gave her husband one last pleading look. "You sure?"

He nodded. "It ain't your time, my love. God knows I wish it was."

She grabbed his hand. He pulled her up out of the snow to a standing position and pointed down the road.

Faith strained her eyes. She still saw nothing through the storm, but she now heard a faint rumbling, the sound of a large truck with chains and a plow. She turned to Russ, but he was gone.

She tried to walk back to the road, but her feet wouldn't move. She forgot that she was still attached to the skis, which were under four feet of powder. She dug down into the snow. The truck was getting closer—this was probably her only chance. She found the binding releases and freed her boots. She stumbled up onto the road just as the truck came into view. She wasn't sure the driver would see her, visibility being what it was, and with that big red blade spewing up snow, so she ran to the other side of the road, out of the way of the snow the plow was kicking off, and waved her arms wildly.

The truck barreled past, burying her skis under even more snow. She would never find them again.

Maybe you were wrong, Russ. Maybe now is *my time. I sure ain't gonna make it anywhere on foot before I freeze.*

But then the truck's brake lights flared; the driver had seen her as he drove by. The snow-and-salt-throwing beast slowed to a stop. Faith stood in shock, half of her thinking she had died there in the snow and this was a modern version of Elijah's flaming carriage come to take her home.

The driver rolled down his window and shouted at her. She went over to him. The man was no blue-collar spirit guide. It was Frankie, one of the deacons from her church.

"What are you doin out here?" he said out the window. "Get in, 'fore ya freeze!"

Faith ran around to the other side and climbed in. She couldn't believe how warm it was in the truck. Only then did she realize how dangerously desensitized she had gotten to the cold. She shivered, the truck's toasty warmth reminding her body how much heat it had lost.

Frankie was staring at her with an open jaw. "Jiminy *crimeny*, sister! What in Sam Hill you think you're doin?"

Faith muttered something unintelligible. Realizing she had made no sense, she took a second to collect herself and let her lips warm up, then she said, "Sorry, Frankie. Thanks for stoppin. It's just... can you get me to the old Hendricks place?"

"What on earth do you wanna go there for?"

"Just somethin I gotta do. Please don't ask me to explain it."

Frankie shrugged. "Whatever floats yer boat, I reckon. Just promise me you ain't gonna be goin out again in this storm by yourself. Mighty Moses an' all of Israel!"

"Believe me," Faith said. "You don't gotta worry about that."

Frankie shifted into reverse, backed up enough to allow for some momentum, shifted back into drive, and continued his cut through the white.

Faith watched the swirling chaos outside her window. *What am I doing?* she thought. *I might really die today. Only by the Good Lord's mercy I ain't still lyin out there in that drift. And now I'm headed straight for a murderer?*

She was foolish, doing this on her own. She should ask this man to help her, to keep her safe.

"Frankie?"

"Yeah?"

Her words stuck in her throat before she could say them. Frankie wouldn't believe her. One word about this fool's errand given to her by her husband's ghost, and he would likely turn right around and make a call to some loony bin up north. Leave out the ghosts, but mention the psychopath—well, that wouldn't make him too jolly about stopping by the old Hendricks place, either. Frankie was a practical man, not one she could call on for this kind of aid. Live or die, this job was hers alone.

"You're a good man," she said. "Thank you."

She glimpsed a figure outside, barely an outline in the whirling white. It was Russ. He lifted a hand to her as they passed. She put her hand up to the glass, and he disappeared.

I'm ready, she thought. *Ain't nothin left for me here, anyhow. See you soon, Russ.*

Chapter Twenty-Four

"Kelsea? Come on out. I need to get you out of here while there's still time."

Kelsea crouched behind the sewing machine. She heard James's footsteps grow louder, and she held her breath.

"Where are you? I don't know if that girl has told you something, but trust me. She's a liar. She's trying to hurt us both."

She exhaled as his calls and footsteps faded farther away. She wondered if she should stay where she was, hidden in the hanging quilts. It was only a matter of time before he checked this room. On the other hand, if she left, he would probably hear her, and even if he didn't, where would she run?

Come on, Kayla. What's taking you so long? Get rid of this bastard!

What if James had done something to Kayla? She had thought she had heard the girl yelling downstairs.

Impossible. You can't kill a ghost. Those things are dead already.

But what did she know about the spirit world? It had been only a matter of hours ago that she had come to terms with the prospect of a soul separated from its body. Surely there were rules she didn't know about. What she did know was that she was grossly unprepared for it to happen to her.

If I live through this, I might need to read up a bit more on this afterlife thing.

"Really, Kelsea. I'm here to help. You don't have to hide from me. What has that thing been telling you?"

His voice was closer again. Kelsea heard a door open and close. He would be here soon. She climbed up onto the chair next to the sewing machine so if he looked under the hanging quilts, he wouldn't see her feet.

"Olly-olly-oxen free!" James called. "Come out, come out, wherever you are."

Kelsea rolled her eyes despite herself. *If I'm ever a psycho killer, I hope I'm a bit more creative than that.*

Clichéd as James's taunt was, it showed that he had given up on pretending to be here to rescue her. Now when he found her, there would be no chance for her to bullshit her way past him in an effort to escape. There was no more time for games.

The sewing room door opened, and Kelsea's heart leapt to her throat. She squeezed her eyes tight and sent up some quick desperate prayers to whatever god or spirit-master or ghost-king was out there.

"There's nowhere to run, Kels."

The voice was frighteningly clear now that he was in the same room with her. Kelsea's heart beat so fast and hard that she was afraid she might die of cardiac arrest before this monster even knew she was here.

The floorboards creaked as James made his way through the maze of cloth. Soon she saw his feet below the quilt directly in front of her.

I have to move.

James's hand appeared, pushing the quilt to the side. Kelsea hopped off the chair and threw it at his face.

The chair hit James in the head just as he pulled the quilt all the way back. He swore and fell backward into another quilt, ripped it off of the pins holding it to the ceiling. Kelsea pulled the quilt in front of her down and jumped onto James while was still stunned and on the ground. Not really sure what else to do, she started stuffing the quilt into his mouth. He gagged and flailed at first, then one of his hands found her hair and yanked hard. She screamed as he pulled her off of him. He let go of her hair to get himself untwisted from the quilts, then he pulled a knife from inside his coat.

"It's really a shame," he said, a drip of blood sliding down from his eyebrow where the chair had broken skin. "The girl was too young. We both were. I'll admit that. But you and I…" He rubbed his mouth. "I thought maybe we had something there."

Kelsea was now between James and the door. She crawled under another hanging quilt and ran for the door, slamming it shut behind her. She heard James yell in rage as he flung the door open and stumbled out into the hall. She ducked into the trophy room. It still smelled of gunpowder and blood.

Kelsea looked around frantically. A shotgun lay in the middle of the floor, next to two used shells. No good. She pulled a scoped rifle from the wall. If the shotgun had been loaded last night—would she be as lucky?

James thundered into the room. No time to check the chamber,

as if I would know how

she spun and pointed the business end at her pursuer. He stopped in shock; then he smiled.

"Come on, Kels," he said. The area above his left eye was swollen, and dried blood was mixing with the sweat trickling down the side of his face. He took half a step back, but he kept his knife up. "You don't want to do that."

"Go away. I'm not kidding." To make her point, she pulled the gun's lever out and back in. *That's what they do in the movies, right?*

James's smile grew wider, and he reneged on his back-step. "No bullets in that rifle, sweetheart," he said. "It's about as good for you as a baseball bat."

"Yeah?" Kelsea said. "Well then, why don't you come on over here and pitch me a good one."

James frowned and then lunged. Kelsea stepped to the side and swung the barrel at his head. The metal only glanced off his ear.

Foul ball, strike one.

But it did throw him off balance, and he tripped into the wall. As he was regaining his balance, Kelsea flipped the gun so that she was holding it by the barrel, the heavy walnut stock now extended. She swung again. James ducked, and the momentum of her swing threw her off of her feet.

Strike two.

She still had the gun firmly by the barrel, but she now lay on the floor. James stood over her, laughing.

Kelsea swung the stock like an axe, hard into James's crotch.

Home run, baby.

He doubled over, grabbing his balls with one hand. He still had a firm grip on the knife in his other, but he wouldn't be focused on using it for the next minute or so. Kelsea dropped the gun and raced from the room. She was sure now that something must be wrong with Kayla, but she didn't have time to find out what.

As she ran down the hall, she heard James screaming at her from the trophy room. "You've done it now, little bitch! You're going down like your twin sister! I got the best of her and I'm going to have the best of you before this is over!"

He was pounding down the hallway after her now. She ran into her bedroom and slammed the door. She moved the dollhouse in front of it. Miniature furniture spilled out all over the floor as it toppled.

That's not going to do much.

"You can't get away from me!" he shouted from the hall. "You've nowhere to run!"

She stood on the bed and tried once more to push the attic door open. It still wouldn't budge.

Kelsea

She didn't have time to ask the creepy attic voice for advice. She needed to get out of here. She pulled the window open and looked out.

The back deck was directly below her. She could see the railing sticking up out of the deep snow. If she could just jump far enough to clear it, maybe the snow would be deep enough to break her fall.

She heard the doorknob jiggle, but the door didn't open.

Thank you, Kayla.

James began to kick the door. Even if Kayla could keep the knob stuck fast, Kelsea knew it was only a matter of a few kicks from this unhinged man before the door would give. She got her feet up onto the windowsill and held on to the sides of the frame. She poked her head out, then her upper body. She took a deep breath and another look at that railing below her. She jumped.

She heard the bedroom door break open, and James tripping over the dollhouse with a stream of curses. But she was already falling, weightless. And she was going to clear the railing. She had time enough for her lungs to tell her she was holding her breath and needed to get some air.

This is either going to be really soft, or really painful, she thought. She didn't have much experience with this snow business.

She hit the white pillow and sank all the way to the ground. The walls of her crater caved in around her. She was buried in darkness, but she was unhurt.

She burrowed forward in a blind frenzy for several feet, then came back up toward the surface. Even standing up at her full height, the snow was piled just over her head. She made a hole and looked back up at the house to see James leaning out the window above her. She turned and pushed through the snow toward the woods.

What is this, Alaska? How can there be so much snow?

She was going nowhere fast. Behind, she heard a soft thump. James was now in the yard with her.

But neither of them were good at pushing through the deep. It was a race of snails.

Adrenaline and furious digging kept Kelsea warm, but she was tiring quickly. It might be easier once she got to the woods, but then where would she go? She fought back tears and hopelessness. James was stronger and faster, and he was probably gaining on her, inch by inch. She had to change her strategy.

She crouched down and burrowed low against the ground again, this time with purpose. This position required her to move less snow, which gave her the advantage of speed. And as claustrophobic as it made her feel, it also gave her the advantage of concealment.

I'll go a few more yards straight out, and then I'll turn and circle back. Maybe I can get back to the house before he realizes where I've gone.

She made better progress this way, but her muscles were on fire, and her hands were burning from constant contact with the snow. She rested for a few seconds and put her hands in her armpits. The silence in her tunnel, though eerie, made her feel alone and almost safe. She was getting used to the tight space, and its unexpected warmth lulled her into a false feeling of security.

Maybe he'll go by without finding me.

She couldn't take that risk—and yet, she was so weak. She couldn't do this for much longer.

I've got to keep going. Got to circle back to the house.

She couldn't hear James, but she knew he could be right behind her—even right next to her—and she wouldn't know it unless she went back to the surface from her tunnel. She wasn't even sure right now if she was still heading away from the house or not. But she didn't dare rise up and give away her location. She kept digging.

Chapter Twenty-Five

"Here we are," Frankie said. "Hoo-ee! That snow sure is deep. I'm gonna drive you straight up to the deck if I can."

"Thanks, Frankie," she said. "I really owe you one."

"Don't mention it. Say, Faith, you sure everything's okay? Something don't seem right about this place. Those windows are all boarded up."

"Yeah. The daughter is, um, doing some renovation."

It was a pretty weak lie, Faith knew, but Frankie looked confused rather than suspicious.

"The daughter?" he said. "Didn't she, um…"

"No, the other one. There were twins. Child Services took other young'un after the accident."

"Oh, wow. I'd forgotten about the other'n. I was what—thirty when that happened? Sad story. Whole thing kinda gives you the spooks, don't it?"

"Don't be so superstitious. I'll be fine. Thanks again."

Frankie nodded.

Faith dropped down from the truck into the snow. It was up to her waist where she landed, and she had to lift her legs as high as her old joints would let her in order to climb the steps to the deck. She turned and waved at Frankie.

"You sure everythin's fine?" he yelled out the window over the diesel engine's loud chugging.

"Yeah, the Hendricks girl is inside. Like I said, I gotta help her with somethin."

"All right. I'll see you later, Faith."

"See you."

Faith watched him back down the driveway the way he came. The tires stuck in the snow once, even with the chains, but he made it back to the road.

Faith was alone now, and totally unsure what to expect. There were high drifts all around the house, but it looked like someone had already made some tracks to the front door. Even those were being softened and filled in by the blizzard, though.

The front door was already cracked open. She walked into the dark living room.

"Hello?" She mentally kicked herself. *Faith, you idiot. If the crazy man is already here, now he knows you're here, too.*

But no crazy man came. Instead, she heard a child crying. She followed the sound to a closed door down the hall.

"Hello?" she whispered.

The crying stopped. There was a sniff, and then nothing.

Whatever was behind that door, it sure didn't sound like someone Faith should fear. She tried the knob, and though she saw no lock on the door, it wouldn't open.

"Don't be afraid, honey. I'm here to help."

The door opened on its own. Faith stepped into the

room and peered in the low light. A young girl stood in the middle of the room.

"What's your name, honey?" Faith said. "Mine's Faith. Come to me, child." She extended her hand in invitation. "I ain't gonna hurt you."

The girl stayed where she was and stared at the woman sulkily.

Faith moved slowly closer. Her eyes, so accustomed to the brightness outside, were still adjusting to the tiny light coming in through the boarded windows. But she saw that the girl's hair was blond, her eyes a bright green. Her face was smeared with a strange black substance that looked like tar or dirty motor oil.

Faith crouched down to the girl's eye level and reached out a hand. The girl flinched back, but did not run, and Faith felt a shock of icy cold as her hand passed straight through the small girl's shoulder.

"Lordy," she whispered. "You're the little dead Hendricks girl."

The girl nodded.

"What was it? Kendra? Kiley?"

The girl hesitated; then she said, "Kayla."

Faith nodded. "Of course, that's right. Listen, Kayla. My husband, Russ—he's been dead for a while now. But like you, he ain't yet flown away to glory. He told me to come here. Said that your sister was in trouble. But not from you."

The girl nodded fervently. "The man is after her. But he trapped me here. He burned something that hurt my eyes, and then he made this circle around me with his white powder."

Faith looked at the floor. There was a circle of white dust around the girl, just as she said. Faith took a pinch and touched it to her tongue.

She almost laughed. "It's just salt," she said.

"Whatever it is, I'm stuck in here, and Kelsea is out there—with *him*."

Faith was reminded of the immediacy of the danger. She brushed some of the circle away with her hands. "There. Now can you get out?"

The girl stepped out of the salt, looking embarrassed at having been bound by such a common substance.

"Where is Kelsea?" Faith said.

"I think they're in the back yard. It may be too late." Dark hatred crawled onto the girl's face. "Let's go."

The girl took off, and Faith hustled to keep up. She put her hand in her pocket and tried to take comfort from smoothness of the gun's handle against her palm.

This is it.

Chapter Twenty-Six

The snow above Kelsea's back broke open; she was exposed. She popped up, hoping she was in the woods, but she found herself standing right in the middle of the yard, in a spot where the wind had blown the snow shallow. James was twenty feet away, in another fairly shallow spot, and he spotted her instantly. His eyes narrowed and locked onto her, and he ran toward her with his knife at the ready.

She was ten feet from the shed. Freezing tears and icy snowflakes stung her cheeks as she tripped toward it. The snow had drifted up against the door. She dug through it frantically, her fingers numb now. She fumbled the door open with barely responsive hands, slipped into the darkness within, and shut the door behind her. It had no lock. She pushed forward blindly, tripped over the lawnmower, and fell.

James threw the door open. The contrast between the white behind him and the shed's shadowed interior cast him as a dark silhouette in the doorframe.

He laughed. She had nowhere else to run, and he knew

it. "You really gave me a workout," he said.

She scooted back, pressed herself against the far wall. "My parents—you said they were good to you," she said, trying to keep him talking until she figured out a plan. "But you killed them. Why did you kill them?"

"They found out. Maybe that ghost sister of yours told them. I don't know. But once they knew, they had to go. Like you." He took a step forward, and the old plywood floor groaned.

"Help!" she screamed. "Kayla! Somebody!"

"Nobody's going to help you, Kels. I *did* call my friend at the police station, you know, to get a feel for what they know. Turns out Coop was on his way out of town for a few days when he stopped by your place. They don't even miss him yet!" He laughed. "And I took care of your sister, too. It was easier than I thought. Shoulda tried the old salt-and-sage trick before I ever thought about getting that dumb priest involved. Now I've got an extra body to figure out how to account for after this is all over."

She looked around the dark shed in desperation. A rusty bow saw hung from a nail on the wall next to James, but there was no way she would be able to get to it. An image came to mind of her father walking across the yard, carrying a Christmas tree over his shoulder and the saw in his other hand, but she was too terrified to appreciate the nostalgia.

The odor of sweat—both hers and James's—was strong, and a strange thought passed through her mind: *I don't want that to be the last thing I smell before I die.*

She kicked the lawnmower, and the handle jabbed James

in his stomach. He bent over, surprised for a second, but then he shoved it back at her with a growl. The rusty metal chassis ran up her shin, and she cried out.

James was stepping closer when a shot rang out. He spun around.

A woman stood on the deck, shoulder-deep in the snow, pointing a smoking pistol at them.

"Now don't you get any closer to the girl," the woman yelled. "I ain't afraid to put a bullet in your sorry ass."

Relief and gratitude flooded Kelsea as James glanced back at her with a look of terror. But then his terror changed into amusement, and the fear came back to roost in Kelsea's gut.

"Crazy old widow," James muttered. He yelled out the door, "You sit tight, Faith! I'm coming for you next!"

Faith fired the pistol again, but the bullet went nowhere near the shed. James pointed at the woman with his knife and looked at Kelsea, laughing as if they were in on the joke together. "You see this? If she could have hit me from there, she would have done it on the first shot. She doesn't scare me."

"*She* might not scare you, but I know *I* do," came a voice from just outside the shed.

Kayla's form passed through the wall and stopped between James and Kelsea. The temperature in the shed dropped by ten degrees.

James's face went white. "You…" He stood there in dumb shock for a second, then he reached inside his jacket and pulled out the bundle of burnt sage.

"Not this time," Kayla said.

She raised her hands, and the carved wooden chains hanging from the rafters came down and wrapped around James's wrists. She pulled his hands up and fastened them tight. James dropped the sage and his knife.

Another chain came down and wrapped around his neck.

The wind picked up. Just below its howl, Kelsea heard a soft chuckle come from Kayla. It made her blood run cold even in her profound relief of deliverance.

The chain tightened steadily around James's neck. He thrashed against his bonds, but to no avail. A vein appeared on his forehead, and his eyes bulged. Then his eyes rolled back, as if he was passing out.

"Oh, no, you don't," Kayla said. The chain around his neck loosened, though his wrists were still held fast. His head drooped down, and he hung there limply.

Kayla walked up to him and rose so that her face was level with his. She lifted his head back up and slapped it with her hands. "Wake up. You're not getting out of this that easy."

James blinked and opened his eyes. He coughed.

"That's better." The chain tightened around his neck again.

"Wait, wait—" James began, before the chain cut off his words.

This time the chain jerked him back and forth as it squeezed. Kayla giggled in delight. The chain rattled faster back and forth, and Kayla forgot her glee for fury. She released an inhuman scream of rage that could never come from the vocal chords of a physical girl. Then the chain stopped and hung loose again, the man kept alive by a strand.

Kayla turned to Kelsea and smiled. "Isn't this fun?"

Kelsea felt sick. "I don't know." She looked at James, purple marks around his neck, barely conscious. "We have him trapped now. Can't we just, like, call—" She was going to say "the police," but then she remembered Kayla's less-than-favorable opinion of the civil servants. The sickening picture of Sheriff Cooper stuck under the ice flashed in her mind again. She would probably never forget that. "Can't we just call for help?"

"*Help*?" Kayla said. Her face renewed its expression of hatred. "No, thank you. I tried calling for help twenty-five years ago. If I learned anything in my short life, I learned how foolish it is to hope for rescue from man or God. Jimmy here is about to learn the same lesson."

It was hard for Kelsea to argue. James had done a terrible thing to Kayla, after all. He deserved this. But she couldn't bear to watch.

The woman who had shot at James appeared in the doorway, wide-eyed and breathing heavily, and put her hands on her knees.

"Come on, honey." She motioned with one hand for Kelsea to come. "Get on outta there before you get hurt."

Kelsea looked at Kayla, who nodded. "She's right," the girl admitted. "My storehouses of wrath are apt to spill. I don't want you near if that happens. You're family."

Kelsea squeezed past James and stepped out into the wind and snow with the old woman.

"Good girl." She enveloped Kelsea in a hug. "You're safe now." She pulled back. "Name's Faith, by the way."

"Kelsea."

"Good to meet you."

The two watched with nauseous horror as Kayla went another round on James's neck.

"I dropped the gun in the snow on the way to you, or else I would shoot him right now, put the poor wretch outta his misery."

Kelsea nodded. She couldn't speak, and she didn't want to watch, but she couldn't look away. Kayla's expression was a strange mix of ecstasy and malice that was all the more terrifying painted on the canvas of a kindergartener's face.

Kayla once more loosened the chain around James's neck. She frowned thoughtfully—a look that seemed to say, *I wonder if this will work*—then she stuck her immaterial hand into James's groin.

He snapped his head back and let out an anguished scream. It sounded like his throat was stuffed with sandpaper from the damage the girl had done to him. Kayla jumped up and down and laughed. Then she lifted herself up to James's face again, and this time she put her own hands around his neck and squeezed. Her face twisted up and her cheeks puffed out in fast angered breaths as she throttled the man back and forth.

Perhaps the direct contact between her hands and his flesh caused her to lose her self-control, for she went on too long and too hard. When she did let go of James's neck, it was too late. He was finally dead.

"No," she said. She slapped his face. "Wake up! I'm not done!" She shot Kelsea a helpless look, then looked back at the dead man hanging by his outstretched wrists. "*Wake up!*" she screamed, slapping him again.

The chains loosened, and James's corpse fell backward. It landed with his upper body halfway out the door, his head in the snow at Kelsea's feet.

Kayla stared at the dead man, stunned, then started to cry. "It isn't enough," she said between sobs. "It wasn't enough."

A voice passed on the wind. Kelsea thought it sounded familiar, but she couldn't make out the words.

But Kayla could, apparently. "No!" she answered. "I'm not ready! There must be something else."

The wind spoke again. Kayla shook her head and pouted and cried.

Then another figure appeared outside the shed. It faded in slowly until Kelsea finally recognized the spirit before her.

"Father Marco!" she said.

He smiled at her warmly. "Howdy, Ms. Hendricks." Then he turned to Kayla. "So."

Kayla sniffed and crossed her arms. "If you've come for an apology, you won't get one. You stood in my way. Now you know what he did to me."

Father Marco said nothing. The girl tried to keep a steely-eyed face, but another tear slid down her cheek. "Go away," she said.

"You stole my life from me, and from those who love me," the priest said.

Nobody spoke. The wind whined and shot stinging crystals at Kelsea's cheeks. She hugged herself tight. Faith looked back and forth from one ghost to the other.

The priest sighed. "But I forgive you," he said. "You can apologize if you want, but you don't have to. Either way, I ain't willin to lose myself by holdin on to a grudge. No matter what you done."

The girl looked to the side, avoiding Father Marco's gaze.

"You see it, don't you?" he continued. "Surely you gotta see what it's done to you, holdin on to that for all these years. Sure, the man was a worm, depraved beyond belief. But look at you. Look how your anger has twisted you all up."

The girl looked back at him. "*Somebody* had to do something! But there was nobody but *me*. I needed vengeance!"

"The Lord says that vengeance belongeth to Him."

"*I was his agent!*" she screamed.

Faith reached for Kelsea's hand.

Please don't set her off again, Kelsea thought, hoping the priest could read her mind.

Father Marco nodded. "Maybe what you say is true. But that was your choice. You could have left it to other means. Instead, you held yourself back from eternal rest to take it into your own hand. And for what? Nothin but hollowness, after all that's said and done." He paused. "And that ain't your only wrong."

The girl bent her head, crying again. He walked to her, bent down, and put a hand on her shoulder.

"Let 'em free," he said.

Through her tears, the girl nodded. Without raising her head, she lifted off the ground and floated slowly up to the house, then through the open bedroom window on the second floor.

The priest looked at Faith and Kelsea. "Come on," he said.

They followed Father Marco through the yard to the house. So many thoughts flooded Kelsea's mind. She had little handle on what was going on; all she could do was follow and see what happened next.

Father Marco led them up the stairs and into the children's bedroom. The attic door was open now, and a folding wooden ladder led up into it. Orange light emanated from above.

Father Marco motioned for Kelsea to ascend.

"Now hold on a quick minute," Faith said. "You sure you wanna be cooped up with that girl again?"

"I think the danger's past," Kelsea said.

Father Marco nodded.

Kelsea climbed the ladder. She brushed a cobweb out of her face as she poked her head through the hole. At the top, she stepped to the side to let Faith up behind her. Father Marco opted to go the ghostly route, ascending straight through the ceiling.

In the center of the empty attic was the source of the orange glow. Kelsea had to shield her eyes from its brightness. It was putting out a great deal of heat. Despite the chill in the house, the attic was cozy, perhaps even too warm.

Kayla stood beside the light, looking at the floor.

"Kelsea," said the light.

Kelsea recognized the voice. It was the voice she had heard on the phone, the voice that had whispered to her from the attic. It was also the voice on the wind outside, the one Kayla had shouted at.

"Sorry," it said. "Let me tone it down a bit."

The light softened, then took the shape of an older man and woman.

"Mom? Dad?" Kelsea said.

Both glowing figures smiled and nodded.

"I don't understand."

Father Marco gave Kayla a hard look. "Tell her," he said.

Kayla looked up at Kelsea. Her shamed and tired face took on years of age. "They tried to talk me out of my wrath," she said. "And they wanted to talk to you. I couldn't let them get in my way, though. So I locked them up here."

Kelsea didn't know what to say.

Kayla looked at her parents, then back at Kelsea, then at the priest. Faith took a step back into the corner and kept silent.

"But he hurt me so *badly*," Kayla said, still pleading her case to Father Marco. "He was a monster."

"I know. But some things aren't up to us to fix. You have to let it go."

The girl nodded. Then she turned to Kelsea. "I'm sorry," she said. She held out her small, ghostly hand.

Kelsea didn't know what to say to all this. But she took her sister's hand and squeezed it, and that seemed to be enough for the girl.

Kayla removed her hand and faced her parents. "You were right," she said. "And I was wrong to keep you from her."

The old couple glowed a little brighter and warmer, and the woman wiped tears from her cheeks. She put her arm around Kayla and pulled her close. Then she looked at Kelsea.

"We didn't want to leave…" she began, choking up. She took a deep breath and started again. "We didn't want to leave until we made right with you."

Kelsea felt a lump form in her throat, along with a stab of anger. *Now* they wanted forgiveness? After all the years she had been on her own, it seemed a little late for apologies. Kelsea tightened her lips.

The couple must have sensed her feelings, as hurt showed on their faces.

"You have to understand," the woman said. "We were so ashamed. After they took you away, we couldn't face anyone, not even you."

"It destroyed us all," the man said. "But we have this chance to salvage what might be left." He stepped to Kelsea and put a warm hand on her face. "You've become so beautiful," he whispered. His eyes were deep cisterns of longing and sorrow and love.

Kelsea started to cry, though her fists were clenched at her sides, still holding on to bitterness.

"Please forgive us," he said. "Not just for my sake, or for your mother's, but for your own. I know we should have found you again. I know your anger is justified. But if you don't let go of it, it will ruin you."

Kelsea looked away.

"Don't push us away, please," her mother said. "Don't push everything away."

Kelsea was furious, yet she knew they were right. Ignoring

her pain, as if by closing her eyes it would all just go away—it was all she had ever done. She felt some brittle forgotten place in her heart crack, seeping out love.

She looked up at her father, and at her mother behind him, who was now holding the hand of her sister. Tears streamed down everyone's cheeks and glimmered in the parents' glow.

"I love you so much, my Little One," Kelsea's father said.

Long-lost memories trickled into her consciousness:

her father reading to the girls, one on each knee, his shirt smelling of pipe tobacco and old books

her mother, pins clamped between her lips, measuring and fitting a dress to her small frame

she and Kayla on Christmas morning, wide awake hours before sunrise, nearly trampling each other in their rush down the stairs, the dollhouse bigger than them both and their eyes widening to match it

lying in bed, hot with fever, her father's cool lips on her forehead, her mother with a cup of soup in her hands

The hard place in her heart broke fully, and she hugged her father. "I love you too," she said. Her mother and sister joined them in the embrace.

"He's about to be taken," the priest said. "Let's go."

Kelsea didn't know what he meant, but Marco and the other spirits descended into the bedroom, so she followed, and Faith came down behind her.

Father Marco was standing next to the open window. Though the wind blew in fiercely, Kelsea felt warm next to her parents' spirits. She looked over at Faith and did a double take when she saw Russ, that redneck she had been so suspicious of, wrapping his arm around her shoulders. Russ winked at Kelsea, and Faith gave her a sheepish smile.

"His soul is waking up to his death," Father Marco said, gesturing toward the window. "Watch."

Kelsea peered out into the storm to see James's wavering spirit pull itself free from its dead flesh prison.

The ghost looked up at the window with a scowl. Kelsea's heart beat faster.

Oh, God, it's not over. He's back.

But a hooded, faceless figure ascended slowly from the ground and hovered next to James. They looked at each other, some wordless communication passing between the two. James shook his head savagely, and his eyes widened in naked terror. The hooded creature took James's wrist, and James screamed as the faceless one dragged him effortlessly underground.

"You see, Kayla," Father Marco said. "He was always gonna pay. All you done was to waste yourself away until you got all twisted up, all for somethin that wasn't your job."

Kayla nodded. "I see that now."

Kayla grabbed Kelsea's hand. Kelsea was surprised to find it was warm now—none of the iciness she had always felt around the girl before.

"What I did to you was wrong," Kayla said. "I wish you had come to know me in a different way."

Kelsea still didn't know how to react to all these revelations or the emotions she was discovering within her. She said nothing, just smiled and squeezed Kayla's hand.

"Time to go home," said Father Marco.

Kelsea's mother, father, and sister held each other as they began to ascend with the priest.

Father Marco looked down at Russ. "You comin?"

"You know, Father," Russ said, his arm still around his widow. "I, uh—if it's all the same to you—I think I still might want to tarry just a while longer yet. I'll be with you by-and-by."

Father Marco nodded. "He'll send for you when it's time."

"He knows where to find me."

Kelsea's parents looked down at her.

"Goodbye, my dear," her mother said.

"Goodbye, Little One," her father said.

Kayla waved and smiled, her parents' glow spreading to her own face.

That's my family, Kelsea thought.

They were beautiful as they departed.

Epilogue

It was a record-breaking storm. Despite the epic last-ditch efforts of Frankie and the rest of the snow removal crew, all roads leading out of the county were closed for three weeks. The governor declared a state of emergency over Tucker, Randolph, Pendleton, and Pocahontas Counties during this time.

The locals took it in stride. West Virginians are of the hardiest sort, and they help their own. The elderly shut-ins received relief from younger family members and neighbors. Churches put together woodcutting crews to gather fuel for people who needed it. The kids and schoolteachers welcomed the extended break from school.

Faith and Kelsea weathered the storm together at the house. Russ was often with them; he mentioned something about "his woods-wanderin days" being over and "doin a little wanderin of the house-hauntin sort." Kelsea half-joked that he had better mean *his* house, not hers, and his ghost-belly shook with laughter. "You know, Kelsea, you remind me of your pappy," he said.

Kelsea missed her flight to LA, of course. She was surprised to find that this didn't bother her.

Every evening, Faith and Kelsea sat in front of a cozy fire under the watchful eye of Mr. Deer. But even the parts of the house that should have stayed cold, like the study with its makeshift plastic window, were always warm. It was as if Kelsea's parents had left a few pieces of their souls behind, so that Kelsea would never be cold again.

Frankie soon showed up on a snowmobile. Apparently he had checked Faith's house to make sure she made it back safely, and when he found it empty, he had headed straight for the Hendrickses' place, fearing the worst. Faith told him what they would tell the police later: that for reasons unknown, James had suffered a break from sanity and murdered the sheriff and the priest, using this property as his killing grounds. He had locked Kelsea in the shed and was planning on killing her later, after he was finished with whatever terrible designs he had on her. Faith had heard that Kelsea was in town and wanted to come give her condolences for her folks' death, and she got there just in time. With the element of surprise, she took James from behind with one of the wooden chains just as he was about to carve Kelsea up in the shed.

Frankie was too shocked and grateful for their safety to consider any holes in this story. The county police that soon followed, also on snowmobile, knew there must have been something more to the story, but they chose to turn a blind eye to it. Like the others in Davis who had clammed up when Kelsea had mentioned the house, these had heard rumors of dark threatening forces surrounding this lot. Whether or not the women's story was true, they knew that neither Faith nor Kelsea were murderers. They accepted the lie and dropped the investigation before it could start. They also managed to keep the story quiet enough to avoid drawing outside media attention. The locals all heard, of course, but knew better than to talk about it with outsiders. The last thing anyone needed was attention from some television show that would inevitably paint the county's inhabitants as a bunch of backward, inbred crazies. West Virginians help their own.

It was a moonless night when the storm finally cleared out for good. Kelsea stepped out onto the deck, which Russ had shoveled out for them. ("This ol' back don't hurt me none now that I don't got any bones," he had said to Kelsea with a hearty laugh. She was mostly used to him now, but she was still struck by the bizarreness of a dead man telling jokes and doing chores for her.) The lights from the ski resort had shut off, but Kelsea found herself glad for this. She looked up at the stars.

Russ and Faith joined her, hand in hand. "There's ol' Orion, lookin back down at us from his huntin grounds," said Russ, almost in a whisper. "And the Li'l Dipper, peekin on up over the mountains to the north. Taurus a-chargin overhead."

These are the lights of the mountain night, Kelsea thought. *These are the night lights of my family's home.*

THE END

Acknowledgements

David Gatewood kicked my butt on the copyedit. Once in a while I tried to kick back, but I think he got the best of me. Any prose that you don't like, blame me, not him, since he lets me ignore his advice sometimes.

Thanks to my beta readers: Aubrey, Ethan, Doug, and Judi. You all helped tremendously. Thanks for reading the sloppy version of my book; I hope you like this version better.

Thank you, Emily, for encouraging me, supporting me, and reading my writing a bajillion times.

Big thanks to all the others who helped me get this story out in its current form, and of course, thank you, reader, for giving me your time.

Author's Note

I named the character of Miles Hendricks after the late Miles Dean, a poet from Fayetteville, West Virginia, a friend of mine. I'm sorry that I couldn't know him longer than I did, for he was always kind and unassuming, and his love for people, words, and West Virginia was immediately apparent upon meeting him. In only name and love for poetry do Miles Dean and Miles Hendricks share any intentional similarities; the rest of Miles Hendricks is of my imagination.

I grew up in Davis. Tucker County is, by far, my favorite place in West Virginia, and probably my favorite place in the world. Unfortunately, I haven't lived there in quite some time. In fact, I wrote the first draft of *Little One* in Wyoming, from what I called "my office"—a little table hidden behind the nonfiction stacks in the Pinedale branch of the Sublette County Library. Discrepancies between the real Tucker County and the area as described in my story are due in part to a faulty memory as well as my taking artistic liberties where necessary. Also, it was hard to do justice to the area when much of the book was tied to Kelsea's viewpoint, which was not always appreciative of my beloved home, especially in the story's beginning. I hope that the reader does not mistake her initial disdain for the Mountain State and its people for my own feelings.

To contact me, or to check on what's new, visit my website:

www.tghuguenin.com

While you're there, you can sign up for my newsletter to keep abreast of new releases and other email-worthy stuff.

If you liked this book, please do me a big favor and leave me a review on Goodreads and Amazon. Again, thanks so much for reading.

—Timothy G. Huguenin
Bartow, WV
2017